DRAGONS AND DREAMSELLERS

Krista Joy

For Daniel
the original poor keeper of time…

WASTE YOUR TIME WISELY...

CHAPTERS

1. The Sound of Ticking
2. A Dragon on the Doorstep
3. Sheridan
4. The Blue Room
5. The Edge of the Otherworld
6. A Cantankerous Ghost
7. A Bottled Dream
8. Father Time Himself
9. The Dreaded Stackhouse
10. What Happens in the Watch Room
11. Danger
12. A Bumpy Ride
13. Bin Rist
14. A Wise Old Dragons Tale
15. Gram-Shank
16. The Duke of Quill
17. The Enchantress of Tempura-Sleus
18. The Nixies of Malice
19. The Tickers Descend
20. Travelling by Dream
21. Jack
22. In the Hall of the Architects
23. Breaking the Fortress
24. The Fourth Ouroboros
25. Mr Grisham Revealed
26. Back to the Watch Room
27. Mr Dreamseller Revealed
28. The Dragons Approach
29. Fire and Ice
30. As it Should Be
31. Back to Reality
32. An Exceptional Keeper of Time

1

THE SOUND OF TICKING

"We're late!"

It was not the wake up call Letisha needed at the crack of dawn on the first day of the summer holidays.

Mum was frantically checking plane tickets as she continued to call, when Letisha finally rolled out of bed, just about dressed and ready to go. Letisha was herded into the car along with her suitcase without a chance to complain. They rolled off the drive and out of the little cul-de-sac before her seatbelt was even fastened.

As they sped along, Letisha glared at the other cars, packed with families going on normal holidays. She closed the window as the rushing wind played havoc with the chaotic mane of curls that often hid her round face, freckled cheeks and curious green eyes.

Letisha was not going on holiday; she didn't even know the person she was being forced to stay with.

"I don't remember Mr Tempus at all," she moaned. "Why are you working too when Dad is already away?"

"We saw Mr Tempus a lot when you were a baby," said Mum. "It was a long time ago. And he was ancient even then…"

"Ugh, he's old as well?" Letisha groaned. It would probably be a crusty old house full of dusty cabinets full of things she wouldn't be allowed to touch.

"He's not that old." Mum echoed her groans. "And you know your father and I have to get the work where we can."

Letisha was used to both her parents doing stints of work away from home; her father, Jack Tate, worked on cruise ships as an entertainer and the summer was a big earner. He often tested new magic tricks on his daughter, much to her embarrassment. She was getting too old to be impressed by simple sleights of hand. Mrs Jennifer Tate had been a singer and dancer once on cruise ships before her daughter was born, having gone back to the stage a few short years ago.

Letisha continued to whine. "Why can't I just come with you?"

"I wish you wouldn't complain so much, Letisha," Mum sighed as they stopped at a set of traffic lights. "Mr Tempus is a nice man. Would you prefer we left you with Aunt Liz?"

Letisha had no answer to that. Aunt Liz was her mother's sister, a frightful woman who taught at the high school she would be moving to after the holidays. Aunt Liz, or Aunt Stackhouse as Letisha called her, loathed children. Unfortunately, her niece was no exception.

She sighed as she gazed longingly out of the rain-spattered window. The sun was rapidly disappearing and a storm was setting in.

"I always forget what a trek it is," Mum grumbled, squinting through the rain.

With the weather suiting her mood, Letisha set her mind; she was quite determined to dislike where she was going.

"You'll come and get me if I don't like it, won't you?" Letisha asked hopefully. "Six weeks is an awfully long time to stay with a stranger."

"I promise you will like Mr Tempus if you give him a chance. He really is a very interesting person." Mum set her jaw and added seriously. "I daresay some time with a watchmaker might do you some good."

Letisha rolled her eyes and got comfortable for Mum's impending lecture.

"Your teacher called before you broke up, and told Dad you'd been late for school almost every day for the last three months. What have you been doing?"

"Nothing," Letisha said quickly. "Sometimes I stop to look at the ducks on the river, or I sit on a bench and listen to the birds singing. I honestly never mean to be late, it's just something that happens. I get caught up in other things!"

"You'll need to be on time when you go to high school," Mum sighed sympathetically. "You just need to be a bit more careful, poppet. Mr Tempus will set you right on track. There's a nice park nearby, maybe he'll take you there at the weekend. You'll have plenty of time for ducks then."

Letisha folded her arms stubbornly, and made up her mind to dislike the park as well as Mr Tempus. It would be a boring old park in a boring old village.

Finally, Mum turned into a small car park with no tarmac. They walked half the length of the single street village to find the shop. The road was adorned with silver birch trees and little green benches dotted with pensioners and ramblers.

Letisha thought how little everyone seemed to be doing. She could not see any children, though she already assumed that if there were any they would be as boring as the village itself. Mum commented how it was a miracle that anyone did enough business to stay open, but Letisha wasn't interested.

"I'm the youngest person here by half a century," she snorted.

"Don't be silly," said Mum. "I'm certain there will be plenty of other children to play with. You might make some new friends."

"In a watchmakers?"

"Don't be so narrow minded, Letisha. Think of it as an adventure; all your friends will be stuck at home over the summer, won't they?"

"Lucy Price is going to Majorca," Letisha replied flatly, deciding that she was right and Mum just didn't want to admit it. "And you're going to the Bahamas. Why can't I go to the Bahamas?"

"Letisha, we've been over this; your father and I don't go on holidays, we go to work. Nobody dreams more than I do about spending the summer together as a family, but money is tight right now." Seeing Mum so frustrated made Letisha resist answering back. She felt a pang of guilt but refused to let it show. Mum carried on regardless. "Anyway, let that be an end to it; we're here."

They stopped at a lane named Covert Street, too narrow for a car to drive down comfortably. Both sides were lined with narrow terraced houses. A house halfway down on the left had a sign hanging above the door. In beautifully hand painted script were the words 'P. Tempus, Master Watchmaker'.

"It's not even on the high street," Letisha whined. "How do people find it?"

Mum ignored her. "Let's have a look at you." She pulled a comb out of her pocket and dragged it through Letisha's tangled hair. She straightened the collar of her coat and rearranged the hood of her sweater, sticking out at the back. "You might've dressed a little smarter."

"My only smart clothes are school clothes," Letisha argued. "And I wasn't going to wear them."

"Well if this place is so empty and boring, who's going to see you in them?" Mum frowned. "Have you got your watch on?"

"What?"

Mum sighed and pulled out a box from her handbag, holding the watch that had been given to Letisha on her eleventh birthday. It had a white face with musical notes for hands, and a black strap with colourful notes running along its length. It had never been worn and was immaculate.

"You'll do well to start wearing this," said Mum firmly, fixing the watch around Letisha's wrist.

Letisha made no response as Mum opened the door of the little shop. The sound of ticking poured out onto the street as they ducked out of the drizzle.

Letisha set down her suitcase as soon as she stepped inside.

"Is that my young assistant?" called a little voice from behind the counter.

"It is, Peter," Mum smiled, looking over to see where he was. As she did, her phone rang. She answered, and went on to ramble about airport schedules and a lot of other things Letisha didn't understand. Mum hung up quickly, "I've only got forty minutes to get to the airport!"

"I'll be right with you, if you could just give me one moment!" called Mr Tempus

"Oh dear," Mum hopped from one foot to the other as she anxiously tried to straighten Letisha's clothes once more. "I do hate charging around like this. Peter, please forgive me but I really must dash. Now, Letisha, you be good and mind your manners. I'll call you when I can but you know it's hard to talk when I'm on the ship."

"Yes Mum," Letisha tried not to show how upset she was at being abandoned in a strange place.

"Don't worry, poppet," Mum hugged her. "Dad and I will be back before you know it. I bet by the time the holiday is over we'll struggle to tear you away from this place. We both love you very much."

Letisha tried to hold back tears, but Mum was fretting too much to notice.

"You'll be good for Mr Tempus, won't you Letisha?"

"Yes, Mum," she barely managed, before she found herself deserted in the shop, the clocks endless ticking concealing Mum's footsteps as she darted back to the car.

2

A DRAGON ON THE DOORSTEP

The clocks, the seemingly endless clocks, were too loud. Mr Tempus was a watchmaker by trade, but apparently he also sold and fixed other timepieces too. The back wall was filled with timekeeping paraphernalia of all types. A handsome cuckoo clock hooted loudly as Letisha stepped further inside. It was ten o'clock on the dot; she was actually on time.

"Ah! There you are!" came the little voice once more, though Letisha could not see its owner. She had become distracted by a collection of shiny pocket watches hanging from their chains over a little gap on the counter. She loved trinkets of any sort. Below the glass counter, more watches sat waiting to be bought, in all shapes and sizes, some with large faces and clear numbers, others tiny and delicate.

Letisha jumped as she felt a pair of sharp eyes on her. They were bright blue, twinkling as if their owner knew the world's greatest secret.
Mr Tempus greeted her holding a length of ribbon in one hand. His fingers were long and the knuckles as wrinkled and bulbous as walnuts.

"I...I..." Letisha stuttered.

"You're right on time," he squinted through gold-rimmed glasses held on seemingly by magic on the end of his long pink nose. "How are you with gift bows?"

"Um..."

"I need to borrow a finger. Come back here. There's a hatch by the grandfather clock. Watch your step."

Letisha lifted the hatch and ducked under, nearly tripping on a step that made her realise that Mr Tempus was perhaps the tiniest man she had ever met. He was almost completely bald but for a little neatly trimmed white hair growing around the sides and back of his head. His beard was perfectly snow white, and he had a neat little moustache above a small, kind mouth. He had a little box wrapped in brown paper on his workbench and was attempting to tie a bow on it.

"It's funny," he went on. "I can repair a mechanism as fine as eyelashes, but I can't tie a bow. 'Got myself into a jolly old conundrum."

Obediently, Letisha took the ribbon and tied a bow first time. She was used to tying bows on her favourite purple boots, so took no trouble in presenting a perfect parcel.

"That's very good," he chuckled, setting the box in a space just big enough on the shelf behind him. "Now, seeing as it's going to be a quiet morning, why don't I show you around?"

Mr Tempus gave Letisha a quick tour of the tiny shop. He showed her his workbench, which he had fitted himself below the window where the light was best. A glass counter was filled with many different treasures as well as trays of replacement watch straps. Shelves had been fitted above the counter, all stuffed with both watches and clocks to be admired, and also labelled orders. They were so high that one would need a stool to reach them. The shop had a distinct woody smell, like an ancient forest on a hot dry day. Every surface was beautifully polished and shone like crystal.

The little watchmaker took pride in his work, with a place for everything and everything in its place. It was the complete opposite to Letisha's bedroom at home. She had never seen so many screwdrivers, some fatter than a finger, some as fine as a hair. Her father wasn't much into DIY unless he was manufacturing a new trick.

Letisha found that every floorboard had its own squeak as she followed Mr Tempus. The faded brown flock wallpaper might have been fashionable when Queen Victoria was on the throne. The shop seemed to breathe like Mr Tempus, savouring every gasp as though it might collapse at any minute. She was careful not to touch anything in case the whole place crumbled.

As they finished their tour, the cuckoo clock called out again; it had taken barely fifteen minutes to look around.
Mr Tempus led Letisha and her suitcase through a little red curtain, into the stockroom. Rows of wooden shelves lined the walls, full of more neat little brown boxes, each one labelled with the same handwriting.
Between the shelves at the back there was a great wooden door, with black iron hinges and bolts. There was also a colossal lock.

"What's through there?" Letisha enquired.

"It's just the back entrance, for deliveries and some of my more unusual guests. But you'll come to see all about that in time. I keep a key on a hook above the door, but you must promise me you won't go out without my permission. Do you understand, Letisha?"

She stared up at a large and rusted key that might turn to dust at any second, but soon became distracted by a rickety staircase leading into the darkness above the shop.

"What's upstairs?" she asked.

"I live upstairs, and so will you for now." Mr Tempus replied quickly. He tapped the bannister affectionately and it squeaked as Letisha saw the dust shake from the stair rods.

She looked around the stockroom again, pondering who in the world would ever manage to sell so many watches, and who would have the time to buy them.

"I'll show you to your room," Mr Tempus said, taking hold of the bannister. "And you can drop off your bag."

Letisha followed Mr Tempus up the rickety, uncarpeted stairs, lugging her little suitcase behind her. It was a battered leather affair much like her satchel, which she carried over her shoulder. It contained all her treasures and she could never be separated from it. She had chosen it from a junk shop, despite what her parents had said about it being ready to fall apart. Like everything Letisha chose for herself, it was odd and suited her perfectly. A dusty smell hung in the air. Mr Tempus led the way onto a bare wooden corridor carpeted with two long shaggy green rugs. To the left, a lonely closed door lay at the end of the darkened corridor, but Mr Tempus turned right towards a lighter set of rooms. Letisha noticed two more rooms along the corridor, whose windows she guessed looked out onto the street.

"You'll be staying in my son's old room," Mr Tempus explained. "So you can leave your suitcase in there."

He stopped and opened the door, which creaked in annoyance as if it had been disturbed from a long slumber. Mr Tempus allowed Letisha to step inside, where she thankfully placed the suitcase down. The room was carpeted and decorated with pale blue paper, grossly out of date just like downstairs. Letisha felt a sense of unease seeping from the walls. Mr Tempus wasn't discreet about leaning anxiously from side to side as if he was eager to get away.

"Is anything wrong, Mr Tempus?" she asked in a small, slightly embarrassed voice.

"Oh!" he cried, as if brought back from a daydream. "No, not at all. Would you be happier up here watching television, or if you prefer you can come back down to the shop and see how things are done?"

Letisha considered his idea; the shop was dreary and dull, but the flat was creepy and not the kind of place she wanted to spend her morning if she was alone.

"I'll come down with you, please," she said, reminding herself that although he was a little strange Mr Tempus had offered to take care of her at the last minute and saved her from her awful aunt.

Mr Tempus found a little stool for Letisha to sit on while he went about his work, describing what he was doing and with which tools. As they sat surrounded by the endless ticking, Letisha began to wonder about what had happened to Mr Tempus's family, as he certainly looked old enough to be at least a grandfather. She had noticed a photograph of a boy hanging on the wall beside where Mr Tempus worked. In the old-fashioned sepia image, the boy had a faint playful twinkle in his eye.

"Who's that?" she asked, secretly hoping he might have grandchildren who would visit. At least then she would have somebody to play with. Mr Tempus was slow to answer her inquiry.

"My dear Toby," he sighed, but did not continue.

Letisha frowned; why did adults have to be such hard work, when all she was doing was making polite conversation? Didn't all adults enjoy talking about themselves?

"He doesn't look much like you."

"No, he was always more like his mother."

"Don't you have a picture of her?"

Mr Tempus paused his work and scratched his chin. His brow wrinkled with the effort of remembering. "Toby was always very serious. I'm glad I have this picture so I can remember him smiling."

Letisha sensed that Toby was sadly long gone from this life, and that he was sorely missed. She decided to hold her questions, left with little to do than lean her head on her hand and sigh as Mr Tempus continued with his work. She wanted to learn more about Toby, but sensed the questions were not welcome. Perhaps she could work at it and learn more later in the week.

She was so bored that when a booming knock came from the back of the shop she jumped from her seat.

"I'll get it," she said, dashing off before Mr Tempus could stop her.

With its huge bolts and little cracks that let in slivers of cold breeze, the back door was a pretty daunting affair. At almost eight feet high, Letisha doubted such a big door was necessary in a seven by six foot room.

As she began to undo the bolts, Mr Tempus called to her from the shop.

"That'll be Sheridan to pick up his order," he said, uncertainty dancing in his tone. "Try not to act too surprised when you open the door."

"What do you mean?" Letisha asked quietly, nervously. She was suddenly aware that perhaps the reason for having a great big door might be all too obvious.

Mr Tempus went on. "I told him you were coming to stay, I suspect he'd like to meet you as well as collect his watch…"
Letisha fetched the stool that she had been sitting on to reach the key. She was just about able to touch it if she stood on her tiptoes. The door was knocked again as she struggled.

"Hang on," She slid the key into the lock, and it clunked as she realised it was already open. "One minute!"
She had no idea who Sheridan was or where his order might be, but decided in a moment of pure madness to open the door anyway, pulling on the great handle with all her might.

Letisha stifled a scream.
A pair of green-scaled feet with chunky clawed toes that were easily big enough to wear the boxes of a large pair of shoes stood before her. They were poking out from beneath an enormous pink belly that gleamed like mother of pearl. A pointed green tail flicked from side to side. Moving up the visitor's body, she saw that he wore a red velvet waistcoat, barely held together by three gold buttons. The gold chain of a watch dangled from the pocket. Out of the waistcoat hung two skinny arms, again clawed at the digits. Letisha craned her neck to look up further, as a long head on a long neck leaned in and came nose to nose, or more specifically nose to horn, as the monster, she decided it was, wanted to get a better look at her. The ears, which were the same mother of pearl pink as the belly, stuck out at a forty-five degree angle to its head, overshadowed by a pair of polished horns. Two pale yellow eyes glinted hungrily.

"Good morning!" The monster grinned. "I believe you have my order, young miss."

3

SHERIDAN

Letisha was stunned silent. As the beast grinned, showing two rows of glinting teeth she could not decide if it was being friendly, or deciding whether she would be better in a pie or a sandwich.

"I'll be with you in just a minute, Sheridan! Letisha, please don't be frightened; Sheridan is one of my best customers!" Mr Tempus called after ushering a customer out of the door. Letisha heard him bolting up and turning the 'open' sign to 'closed' as speedily as possible.

He joined her in the stock room, pulling the red curtain across the doorway that at this point divided reality and the strange situation in which Letisha found herself. By this time the beast had his tail coiled round the back of her so she could not escape without tripping over it. He was quizzing her about watches.

"I am an expert and collector of all fine timepieces," he said, since she assumed it was male. He also had a lisp, which she credited to his long, salmon-pink tongue. "Do you own any time pieces?"
Trembling, Letisha held up her wrist and showed him the watch her parents had given her. It was still immaculate, having only been worn for a few hours. She tried to stop her hand from trembling, concerned it might be bitten off.

"Letisha," said Mr Tempus formally, placing a hand on her shaking shoulder. "Meet Sheridan."

"Charmed, I'm sure," said Sheridan, examining Letisha's watch with great interest. He clearly had no idea he was causing so much alarm. "What manner of material is this?"

"P-plastic," Letisha managed.

"Oh! Plastic," Sheridan repeated with interest. He then turned to Mr Tempus and said, "Mr Tempus, I was thinking, perhaps I could commission a piece made with this plastic."

"In good time," said Mr Tempus, and offered a hand to shake. In doing this he lured Sheridan away from Letisha. "How are you?"

"Absolutely splendid, thank you very much."

"And your uncle?"

"He's very well, too. Is my order in today?"

"As promised," Mr Tempus said, going directly to a box on a shelf and pulling it out. It was large in his nimble little hands. He fumbled slightly to remove a huge brass pocket watch, easily as big as a tea saucer. Its surface was decorated with two intertwined snakes, whose green enamelled bodies glittered in the light. A red garnet glinted in each eye.

"'Good as new," said Mr Tempus. "Though I'm not sure how you got teeth marks in it in the first place."

"For once, 'twas not my fault! I said to Uncle Sigmund 'these garnets are so splendid,'" said Sheridan, taking his watch in one hand but still keeping his yellow eyes firmly on Letisha. "'Like bits of candy', and…well you know how Uncle takes things literally."

"Ah," said Mr Tempus understandingly. He still had his hand on Letisha's shoulder. She could almost feel the guilt radiating from his body. She was still uneasy, but comforted by the fact that Mr Tempus seemed to know how to pacify Sheridan.

The dragon put his newly repaired watch away. "Now tell me Mr Tempus, when did the young lady arrive?"

"Oh, of course, how rude of me. Sheridan, meet Letisha, the daughter of some friends of mine. You just got here, didn't you, my dear?"

"I was hoping to meet you!" Sheridan exclaimed, as Letisha gingerly shook the beast's gigantic hand. He pumped her arm up and down with enthusiasm. "I hope I didn't frighten you; I am not nearly as scary as I look!" Sheridan blushed slightly, and then he whispered, "Though I did neglect to polish my horns this morning."

"Don't worry about it." Letisha stammered, still terrified despite all the formalities. "You're a…a dragon, aren't you?"

Sheridan looked shocked. "You say that as though you have never seen a dragon before!"

"Well, I haven't…" She was amazed at how normal the situation was to Mr Tempus.

"Well!" Sheridan cried cheerfully, clapping his hands. "I hope I can set a good example. Dragons are the most well-mannered creatures in all the worlds!"

"I'm sure they are," Letisha said. She was still convinced that he would eat her given the chance.

"So," Sheridan went on, as she realised he was trying to make polite small talk. "Tell me about your watch, Letisha. Is it an antique?"

"I don't think so. My parents gave it to me a year ago, but I've never worn it before."

"Sacrilege!" Sheridan exclaimed. "Such a piece should be worn and loved. I am never without a watch! Sometimes I wear four all at the same time!"

"Well I'm wearing it now," she defended herself.

"Better late than never," Mr Tempus added with a chuckle.

"I suppose that's a start," Sheridan shrugged. He then whipped out his watch, - a shining gold creation with its back engraved with an intricate design - and exclaimed, "Crumbs! I'm late!" With that, he turned to the door. "I must apologise for rushing off, but I have lots to do! Thank you for my watch, Mr Tempus! I shall be back to see you about my commission!"

Sheridan thundered out of the storeroom and off onto the little white wooden porch that sat beyond the back door. Letisha had failed to notice it before, though she didn't really believe that the dragon had ambled off the street without being noticed or screamed at.

With a running jump, Sheridan snapped out a pair of pink wings that shimmered in the sun. He soared up and away into a beautiful blue sky, waving with one hand and clutching the box of his newly mended watch in the other. Despite his hulking great body, he was graceful in flight. Letisha waved back, suddenly elated.

"Sorry about that," Mr Tempus apologised. "I wasn't sure how to warn you that my best customer was a dragon."

"He was...nice," she managed, feeling as if she might never recover from the shock. "I've never met a dragon before."

"I don't suppose you expected you ever would," said Mr Tempus, still sounding a little embarrassed. "Close that door for me, will you Letisha. It gets so cold in the Otherworld,"

Letisha did as she was told, but not before snooping outside. In the distance, she could see a blue mountain range crowning the landscape, and in front of that a series of snow-capped hills and dotted with skeletal trees. The sky was clear and blue, with the slightest hint of pink at the tips of the mountains. She realised she could see her breath, and shivered; something strange was afoot. It wasn't that cold at the front of the shop, she thought, closing the door and pulling the bolts across. Her cheeks were burning as she turned back to the stockroom.

Mr Tempus was standing at the bottom of the stairs when she turned.

"I think you'd better come upstairs. Do you like soup? I made it especially."

Letisha's stomach rumbled.

"Yes, please," she said.

4

THE BLUE ROOM

Letisha could not help her mouth watering as Mr Tempus stood over a little old stove and stirred the contents of a silver saucepan. He had led her upstairs and into the merry little kitchenette in silence, indicating that she should take a seat with a simple gesture. After a few moments of heating he ladled soup into china bowls, passed one to Letisha, and sat down with his own.

"Please help yourself to bread; I baked it fresh this morning," he said, and then paused over his soup. "I admit I should have warned you about the back door."

Letisha tried to look as if a dragon on the doorstep was commonplace, but she knew she was in shock.

"Some things in this world are hard to explain," Mr Tempus went on, "But things in the Otherworld are even harder. My house, as normal as it looks, is in fact a Portal, and that is how many of my customers visit me."

"I didn't think Sheridan strolled in off the street." Letisha managed.

"He's harmless," Mr Tempus was as hungry as Letisha was, but apparently decided that explaining things was more important. Letisha was itching for him to get on with it. "What I am trying to say to you is that living here has placed me as a guardian. Only I know how to unlock the door, and unless it is unlocked in a certain way, it will only open onto the entry behind the house in this world. Does that make any sense?"

"Sort of," Letisha said, very slow to believe anything she was being told. "But I opened the door, Mr Tempus, it was unlocked."

"I was expecting Sheridan, as he often sends ahead to let me know he's coming. We use a telegraph so I know to keep the shop empty for when he arrives. He has been a customer of mine for many years. I'd like to invite him up for tea, but…well, this house isn't made to support his sturdy posterior."

Letisha laughed.

"A portal is a grave responsibility, and not to be played with. I don't mean to frighten you, but sometimes there are unsavoury characters about, and I wouldn't want them to wander through and into this world. Gone are the days where dragons walked freely between."

"Do you remember those days?" she asked hopefully.

Suddenly Mr Tempus seemed even older than before. His shoulders sloped wearily even as his tired eyes twinkled. "Oh no, that was hundreds of years ago, my dear, just a little before my time,"

"Oh," she said shortly.

"You seem very calm about hearing this information," said Mr Tempus. "Are you quite alright?"

"Do my parents know about the Portal?"

Mr Tempus cleared his throat. "This is our secret now, Letisha. Do you understand?"

"I don't think my parents would have allowed this if they knew about Sheridan. They're afraid to let me near the oven at home, let alone a dragon."

"I'm sure they'd find him quite agreeable if they knew him. But we don't have to tell everybody everything. How's your soup?"

"It's good," she said with her mouth full.

"Sheridan's own recipe. Never let anyone tell you dragons are savage creatures; they are wise and gentle."

Letisha smiled. Already she was beginning to see a side to Mr Tempus she hadn't expected. She was desperately trying to dislike him as she had promised herself earlier, but it was proving difficult. Frankly she would be a fool not to get on his good side, unless she wanted to spend the summer being bored to death. Not only that, his cooking was far superior to anything she ever had at home, since her parents rarely made the time to try anything new.

Still, the idea that an 'unsavoury character' might wander through made her nervous. Equally, if the dragons were gentle and harmless, what shape could the real danger possibly take? Mr Tempus relaxed a little, and was shovelling his soup down hungrily when Letisha spoke.

"What kind of things might come though, then? Who lives on the other side of the Portal?"

"Oh, I suspect you'll see soon enough," he said, chewing. "I wouldn't want to ruin the surprise."

*

While Mr Tempus cleaned up after lunch – a task he insisted on doing alone even though Letisha offered to help – he suggested she take a proper look at her new room. Letisha had lived in the same house all her life, so a new bedroom was something of an adventure. Or at least it would have been before she had met a dragon. She firmly decided that she would not be afraid of Sheridan the next time he came to visit, or at least she would hide her fear.

The cold of the tiny box room hit her as soon as she entered. The freshly made bed was covered with a crisp antique quilt, the furniture simple if not dated. Letisha shivered; it did not feel like July. Perhaps Mr Tempus opened the window to freshen things up before she arrived. On pulling back the white net-curtains she found the little sash was firmly shut and bolted against the plummeting rain outside.

She felt eyes on her, and assumed Mr Tempus had finished washing up and was ready to go back downstairs.

"Could we please light the fire if it's still cold in here tonight, Mr Tempus?" She asked, unbuckling her suitcase.

No reply came, so Letisha turned to the door to see that she was quite alone. She shuddered, rubbing her arms to muster a little heat.

Mum had firmly told her to pick up after herself, so she decided to put her clothes into the wardrobe. Letisha abandoned her plan as she found it still full of clothes. She sighed and tried the squeaking drawers in the desk, and found they too were still full of personal belongings that she didn't care to meddle with.

She noticed a shelf above the bed, packed with books about natural history and gardening, and other boring things. Apart from the nightstand there was no room to put any of her own things, as if she was sharing the room with an invisible occupant.

She took her toothbrush and a bar of soap out of her bag, and set them on the nightstand next to a little blue lamp. She noticed it was much newer than everything else, as if it had been put in just for her. It was as if the rest of the room had been persevered for display in a museum.

Letisha established that she did not like this room. The rain thundering against the glass created a din that filled the lonely space. She felt as if the walls were closing in on her and forcing her from the room. She jumped as the wind howled down the chimney and floorboards moaned beneath her feet. A figure in the doorway made her scream.

"What on earth is the matter?" Mr Tempus said, drying his hands on a dishtowel. "That wind's certainly picking up. I daresay this old building lends itself to the wild imagination of a young girl."

Letisha nodded, embarrassed. "You just took me by surprise."

Mr Tempus chuckled. "'Terribly sorry. There's nothing to worry about on this side of the door so you needn't be so jumpy. It's just you, me, and the old house," He affectionately tapped the doorframe, and was met with the groaning of the wind. "I keep the back door locked when I'm upstairs, so you can sleep soundly tonight."

Letisha tried not to look so sullen, as she didn't believe him in the slightest. As they left to go back down to the shop, the room continued to moan and creak in the wind. Letisha wouldn't be rushing back before she had to.

5

THE EDGE OF THE OTHERWORLD

Letisha opened her eyes to the pattering of rain against the window. It was her first morning at the shop. Somehow she had managed to sleep through the night without being spirited away by some horrible poltergeist. Outside it was light, but the morning was dismal and grey.

Mum hadn't rung to let her know if she had arrived yet. The call could come eventually but Letisha had become used to being forgotten about for brief periods of time.

Despite a faint urge to go back to sleep, Letisha also felt compelled to get up. She pulled on a pair of socks, as she hadn't felt the need to pack slippers in the middle of summer. A hat and scarf were always part of her eccentric ensemble, come rain or shine, but she had neglected slippers. She slid out of bed, amazed that the floor didn't moan and give her away.

The house was dark and silent, all but for the endless rain outside. Letisha picked her way along the rugs of the corridor, convinced they would muffle any squeaks. As if something called to her from the shop, she made her way to the staircase.

Letisha was struck with dread, but also awe, as a figure moved about inside the stockroom.

The back door was wide open, the invader oblivious to the idea of being caught in the act. Strangely, Letisha found she was not afraid of this figure; it wore a cape that glistened like quicksilver. Pale, bare feet poked out of the bottom, flitting over the boards without a sound. It was exploring the rows of shelves with slender fingers, moving in complete silence, with all the grace of wind across water. Letisha questioned if she was dreaming, as the figure glowed as if steeped in moonlight. It was almost as if the intruder had stolen all the light and brought it into the shop.

She moved closer, despite her common sense telling her to stay well back. This intruder was nothing compared to a dragon, after all. As she took a step down, she realised that the back door was open to the Otherworld.

Letisha felt surprisingly calm, something she hadn't felt since Mum had abandoned her the previous morning. Perhaps, like Sheridan, the intruder wasn't what it seemed; it was merely another customer.

"Excuse me," Letisha said timidly. "I don't think the shop is open 'til nine."

The figure turned, and Letisha saw it was a woman. She was an elf-like creature, with a round pale face and exquisite features. A mass of shimmering white hair was about to erupt from under her hood.

"Oh, I do beg your pardon," she said in a voice that almost glistened as she did. "Go back to bed now, little one. You must be sleepwalking."

"I'm not sleepwalking," Letisha maintained, despite an urge to do as she was told and return to bed. "You're trespassing."

The woman turned fully, revealing a silver heavily corseted dress beneath her cape.

"Are you a ghost?" Letisha managed, realising that perhaps this was what one classed as an 'unsavoury character'. The feeling of dread she had been having in her room suddenly made sense; the shop and the flat above was haunted. Perhaps Mr Tempus wasn't even aware of it, although it might explain why he didn't exactly want for company.

"A ghost indeed," laughed the woman. "What a ridiculous accusation!"

"Shush!" Letisha whispered. "You'll wake up Mr Tempus, and then we'll both be in trouble!"

"If I was a ghost, my child, then why would I need to pick the lock to open the door into your world? Would I not simply walk through?"

"I suppose you would," Letisha shook her head, unable to make sense of the situation. She felt groggy, as though the woman's suggestion of more sleep had planted ideas in her head.

The invader looked to be done with her business, having continued to check the shelves as she talked. Letisha was powerless to stop her.

"Then what are you, if you aren't a ghost?"

"I am an Enchantress," stated the woman. "And who might you be? Are you a friend or foe of Peter Tempus?"

The enchantress turned to Letisha, waving her hand about her head as she did so. A white staff topped with a glowing orb appeared as if plucked from the air. She pointed it menacingly at Letisha.

"I'm staying with him over the summer. So friend, I suppose."

"Oh," said the enchantress. "Then you may call me Selena. Do you have a name?"

"Letisha."

"Of course," the enchantress laughed. "I should have known. I am an old friend of Peter; we go a long way back. Though he wouldn't admit how long, I can tell you."

Letisha decided this foolishness had gone on long enough. "What are you looking for?" she asked.

The enchantress shrugged. "Nothing that I seem to be able to find here. Still, I suppose Peter wouldn't label it. He's not nearly that stupid."

Letisha began to back towards the stairs. Enough was enough; it was time to alert Mr Tempus to the presence of this peculiar visitor.

"There really is no need to be afraid," Selena was now standing by the back door, opening it fully into the Otherworld. Her body cast a moonlight glow on the wood. "Would you like to see?"

Letisha felt her curiosity welling, though she was growing tired of people telling her not to be afraid. So far there was plenty to be afraid of if she listened to her common sense. Although she hadn't been forbidden from looking outside when Sheridan had left, she hadn't dawdled because of the unnatural cold. There was much about this world that she did not know, but wanted to.

Still, the idea of doing anything this enchantress invited her to do made her quiver with both excitement and fear. She had been exposed to more adventure in the last twenty-four hours than in the rest of her life.

"Honestly, I don't bite," Selena whispered, holding the door open.

"I don't think I'm supposed to," Letisha admitted, though she found she was unable to resist craning her neck to peek around the frame. The world beyond was in the midst of an icy gale, thrashing the trees and a few brave birds with sleet.

"Did Mr Tempus say that?"

Letisha shook her head, the wind creeping in to blow her hair about her face and shoulders. It was already knotted from tossing and turning in her sleep, but she feared the wind would make it worse. She would be forced to comb it out herself as Mr Tempus couldn't possibly be expected to put up with such nonsense. She pulled the length of it over her shoulder and held it there.

"He said unsavoury characters might wander through."

Selena shrugged. "I'm sorry if I gave you that impression."

As Letisha began to apologise, she suddenly realised that she was no longer standing in the relative safety of the stock room, but next to the enchantress on the little porch. Every fibre of her body told her that an enchantress was basically a witch, and all witches were bad. Rarely did circumstances dictate otherwise, but this woman was not what she expected a witch to look like. It did not feel like early morning, but midday perhaps in late October. Still in her pyjamas, Letisha shivered.

"What were you looking for?" she asked again. Selena seemed to have quite forgotten she had company.

"Something important," the enchantress replied. "I believe Mr Tempus had it once, and I'm sure he would have known what it was."

"Perhaps I could pass a message on for you," Letisha suggested helpfully. "I could tell him when he gets up and he could give you a ring…"

The enchantress chuckled at Letisha's innocence. "We don't have many telephones in the Otherworld. I certainly wouldn't want one anyway."

"Then ask him yourself," Letisha said, noticing a distinct lack of telegraph poles on the landscape; it wasn't at all like the countryside of her own world. She wondered just exactly how the telegraph Mr Tempus used to contact Sheridan actually worked.
She wanted only to be helpful but the enchantress was beginning to try her patience.

"It is impossible," Selena went on. "There are laws preventing Peter… Mr Tempus and I from meeting."

"It is because you're an enchantress?"

"That's one way of putting it. I fear it would put all of us in danger if he even saw me. And now that you have seen me…"

"Am I in danger too?"
Selena turned to Letisha, her face stark and serious. She felt fear ripple up her back, along with the wind from the Otherworld. "Not if you can keep a secret; you must promise not to tell anyone you have seen me."

"I promise." Letisha said slowly. In the middle of nowhere, there wouldn't be anybody to blab to even if she wanted to.

"Good. Then we can be friends. If you ever find yourself out near Tempera-Sleus you must call in on me. I'd love to have you for dinner."

"So witches do eat children!" Letisha cried, having misunderstood the invitation.

Selena laughed. "Who even said I was a witch? I certainly didn't. And who told you that? The Brothers Grimm?"

Letisha shrugged.

"What a pair of nosey trouble makers they were. Telling silly tales about the oddfolk. It's all nonsense. Anyway," she rearranged the folds of her dress, preparing to leave. "I think I've done all I can here. Just remember your promise, Letisha. You must not tell Mr Tempus, for his own sake; the consequences could be dire."
Letisha gulped; perhaps Selena was trouble after all.

"Are you afraid of me, child?" Selena grinned with perfect teeth. The air of a lioness stalking a deer lingered about her. Letisha had no intention of being breakfast. Just once, she told herself, lazing in bed would have been beneficial.

"If you wish you were back in bed, I can sort that for you," whispered the enchantress. She banged her staff once on the floor, and then pointed a gloved finger at Letisha. Little beads of white light appeared around her as she began to disintegrate into the morning. Letisha could not fight her heavy eyelids any better than she could comprehend the feeling of falling backwards. Selena's words echoed.

"Sweet dreams."

6

A CANTANKEROUS GHOST

Letisha started awake with the words 'sweet dreams' still ringing in her ears. She glanced at her watch and saw that it was a little after half nine. She was back in bed, with no idea whether she had been dreaming, or had actually woken up early and made her way downstairs to find an enchantress meddling in the stockroom. One thing was for certain; something sinister was going on in the little house.

She dressed quickly while arguing with herself about the probability of meeting an enchantress in the stockroom. She rarely remembered her dreams, so she found it unlikely that she would be able to invent somebody like Selena and remember her so vividly.
She was no more decided as she brushed her hair, more tangled than usual. A smudge on the mirror distracted her, so she lifted her hand to wipe it away. As she did so, the smudge appeared to grow, as if she had breathed on the glass.
 Letisha leaned back and frowned; she was holding her breath intentionally, so as not to add to the smudge. Her jaw dropped as letters began to write themselves into the smudge.
      "T.T," Letisha stammered aloud. She then slapped her hairbrush down on the desk and growled. "Mr Tempus is lying; if this place isn't haunted, then I'm a giraffe!"

Mr Tempus didn't seem fazed by Letisha's late rising. He had laid things out for breakfast as if he expected it.
      "Good morning, Letisha," he chirruped over the chime of the clock as she entered the shop. She had brought a bowl of cereal with her. It was almost half ten.
      "'Morning," she replied quietly.
      "I trust you had a comfortable first night? Oh good, you found breakfast. Your parents would never forgive me if I didn't make sure you were comfortable."
      "I was very comfortable. Only…"
      Mr Tempus turned. "What is it?"
      "I wanted to ask you something, but I'm not sure how to do it without getting myself or anyone else in trouble."

"Oh my, that does sound serious. I can keep a secret, you know," he winked.

"I don't doubt that," Letisha said, deciding she needed to approach the situation rationally. "Do you believe in ghosts, Mr Tempus?"

He chuckled, and she felt silly. "Don't tell me you still think this old place is haunted, Letisha."

"Well, I had a peculiar feeling last night. And then again this morning"

Mr Tempus tapped a pencil on his lower lip, so seriously he might be contemplating the meaning of life.

"As it happens," he replied finally. "I do believe in ghosts. I mean we're all haunted by something, aren't we? I noticed you haven't made any mention of the dreaded Aunt Stackhouse since you arrived, for example."

"Who told you about that?"

"Your parents said she was quite put out when they didn't send you to stay with her, and she insisted on dropping in to make sure I wasn't using you for slave labour."

"What?!" Letisha could hardly believe her ears. She was convinced she had escaped the old bat for at least the summer holidays.

"Don't worry, we'll cross that bridge when we come to it."

"Aunt Stackhouse isn't a ghost," Letisha tried to steer the conversation in the proper direction.

"No, you're right. She's more like a witch." Mr Tempus giggled. Letisha found herself laughing along, as Aunt Stackhouse was nothing like the witch she had supposedly met last night, even though she was definitely more frightening and not half as interesting. Mr Tempus straightened up.

"I do believe in ghosts, Letisha. But I can assure you this place isn't haunted, even though it might seem that way sometimes."

Letisha sighed, feeling she had gained nothing. She wanted to be told that yes, there had been sightings of a mysterious White Lady, who appeared in and out of dreams and made curious threats to those foolish enough to engage her. Or who left enigmatic letters on mirrors for no good reason. Instead, Mr Tempus was as cagey as ever.

"Oh!" he cried suddenly, making Letisha jump a foot off her stool. "Could you fetch something out of the back for me?"

Letisha was sent into the stock room, Mr Tempus pointing towards the little stepladder so that she might reach a specific box of screws. He had completely discarded their earlier conversation, despite the fact that it had obviously stirred something in him. Letisha was convinced he knew something and simply wasn't letting on, if only to keep her curious enough to behave herself. She could not shake the feeling of discomfort as she searched for the screws Mr Tempus had asked for. He had written the name on a scrap of paper, which she dropped in shock as a stern voice spoke.

"Well, this simply will not do."

Letisha turned, expecting to see the voice's owner, but the room was empty. Only the faint sound of Mr Tempus humming filtered through. Letisha called out to him,

"Did you say something, Mr Tempus?"

"No, dear," he called back between hums.

Letisha shivered, noticing that the room had become incredibly cold. Initially she thought that the back door might be open, but found it was bolted tight against any intruders.

"Stop letting your head run away with you," she said to herself out loud.

"They say," whispered the voice, "That talking to oneself is a sign of madness."

Letisha frowned, "I should say a voice in my head is a sign of madness too."

With that she spun round, suspecting a customer had sneaked back into the storeroom and decided to give her the run around.

"I'm not afraid of a voice," she mumbled to the room.

"Oh dear," the voice sounded very angry. The air became even icier, as the light bulb popped and plunged the room into darkness. Only the yellow light from the shop came through a crack in the curtain, where dust particles danced in the air. Out of the corner of her eye, she also saw movement to her left. "Then what are you afraid of?"

At that moment the curtain flew open, and Mr Tempus came in, along with the light and warmth of the shop.

"Good heavens, did I bury that box so well in here…" Mr Tempus trailed off as if he smelled something in the air.

"I don't want to alarm you," Letisha shuddered, "But I think there's somebody in here."

"Ah," Mr Tempus mumbled calmly. He then spoke a little loudly, as if addressing the ceiling. "You owe me a new light bulb, Mrs Grisham's Ghost. There will also be a charge for scaring my young friend."

"Oh poppycock," said the voice, and the light popped back on. "I can't see how that useless little urchin can provide the kind of service I am deserving of. Have I not lived my life and earned the respect of the dead, Peter Tempus?"

Mr Tempus rolled his eyes. "Yes, Mrs Grisham's Ghost."

"That's right. You ought to know better," the voice prattled on, as a vaguely human form began to materialise in the middle of the room, swirling in a blue-grey mist beginning at the floorboards and ending about half a foot below where Letisha stood on the steps. "Honestly it's not enough that nobody heard me knocking, now I have to waste time materialising as well," complained the voice.

Mr Tempus remained stern, yet respectful. "I have a guest, Mrs Grisham's Ghost, and it is only out of manners that you should be introduced properly."

"Indeed," said the voice sharply, as a pair of grey, barely visible naked feet stood on the boards. Coming down the steps as she thought she should, Letisha was near enough face to face with a gaunt woman of late middle age, with wild white-blonde hair and blue eyes ringed with grey. The woman wore a nightgown blotched with mud and grass stains. She was so stern she seemed to spit ice as she spoke.

"Well, girl?" she spat with a mouth so puckered it resembled a hen's bottom. "Introduce yourself, why don't you?"

"Letisha Tate," she said, amazed that any words left her mouth at all.

"What a peculiar name. And so badly dressed," said the ghost, taking a strand of Letisha's hair disdainfully in one hand. Letisha frowned, but let her continue. "I am Mrs Grisham's Ghost. I was Mrs Grisham once, but now I have passed on I am Mrs Grisham's Ghost."

"But surely you have not passed on," Letisha argued. "If you are still here. And you are still you."

Mr Tempus put his palm to his face, knowing how belligerent Mrs Grisham's Ghost could be. She would not take kindly to being challenged.

"I have passed on from being human, child. It will happen to you one day."

"Might we move on to a less morbid subject?" Mr Tempus suggested. "Mrs Grisham's Ghost, what can we do for you today? The usual polish, I presume?"

"Yes, yes," said Mrs Grisham's Ghost, still eyeing Letisha suspiciously as she handed over a gold locket on a chain to Mr Tempus. Despite her iridescent hands, it was quite solid.
Mr Tempus left with the locket to fetch a cloth. Letisha was alone with the ghost.

"And how did Mr Tempus end up with a scoundrel like you working under him, hmmm?" She narrowed her eyes.

Letisha folded her arms; Mrs Grisham's Ghost was not nearly so agreeable or accommodating as Sheridan, and certainly more frightening. "I am not a scoundrel. Mr Tempus is taking care of me over the summer while my parents are working. And I'm not badly dressed either, thank you very much. I'm expressive."

The ghost snorted. "Taking care? What nonsense! Don't children go to school anymore? They went to school in my day."

Letisha came to the conclusion that Mrs Grisham's Ghost liked the sound of her own voice, so asked; "And when was your day?"

"The best era of all, child, under her Royal Highness Queen Victoria herself, and the day of the great empire! Oh," she went on, "What an era it was, when ladies were delicate, and gentlemen were charming, and my husband and I threw fabulous parties!" The ghost blithered as though it were a relief to remember.

"And where is Mr Grisham?" Letisha asked.

Mr Tempus re-entered with the gleaming locket, which he handed to the ghost.

"Regrettably, Mr Grisham and I never found each other in the afterlife." She showed Letisha the image in the locket, of a pale man with sharp features. He had white hair and eyebrows like icicles, and glared right out of the photograph. He and his wife looked well matched. "He was my true love, you know."

"I'm sorry, Mrs Grisham," said Letisha, noticing that Mr Tempus looked as though he was about to choke. The ghost's face clouded over.

"Stupid child! I am not Mrs Grisham. Mrs Grisham is dead and buried and rotten to the bones. I am Mrs Grisham's Ghost. Do you understand?"

"Yes, Mrs Grisham's Ghost." Letisha peeped, looking at her feet and feeling about four inches tall.

"Good," said the ghost, and turned to Mr Tempus. "Thank you, Peter, excellent work as always. Mr Grisham is looking his best again now. I'll take my leave. And," she added in a loud whisper, "I suggest you take some time to better train your staff in customer service!"

With that, she disappeared in a puff of shimmering smoke.

Mr Tempus found the screws he had originally asked for before they sat down in the shop where he continued to work.

"You needn't worry about Mrs Grisham's Ghost," he said, tightening a tiny screw with a little grunt. "She's like that with everybody."

"Really?" Letisha said, uninterested. She had been sufficiently put off the back door, having been scared, insulted and lectured in under five minutes by a complete stranger.

"Don't take it to heart. She's a crotchety old bird, obsessed only searching for Mr Grisham. It's a bit of a mystery, actually."

Mr Tempus gave the watch a final polish, and popped it into the little velvet gift bag that Letisha handed to him. He was very particular about presentation.

"Where's the mystery?" asked Letisha. "She died, and he didn't. I don't blame him for avoiding her, frankly."

"Now, now, love is blind, my dear. Mrs Grisham's Ghost once told me that she last remembers leaving the house to find Mr Grisham after he had been hunting. They lived on the moors, you see, and he liked a good shoot. She was frightened for him, so she followed tracks in the snow onto the moors. She never made it back alive. All she has now is that locket. She doesn't hate anyone, really. She's just heartbroken." He said this as if his own heart was broken, sadness teetering on the edge of his voice for just a moment. He then continued in a more cheery tone. "Why don't you go and fetch us something for lunch from the bakery up the road?"

He opened the till with a bang, and handed her a ten pound note.

Letisha looked at the grandfather clock. "But it's only eleven thirty."

"I know," he said. "But there are certain things I need to do, and I know your parents wouldn't be happy with me if I let you help."
Letisha stood, disappointed, and went to fetch her coat. When she returned, Mr Tempus was removing the more valuable items from the window and pulling the blind down.
She bid him farewell and waved as she passed the window. Why was he eager to get rid of her?

7

A BOTTLED DREAM

Three days passed without incident, though Letisha still felt a presence in her room as she attempted to sleep, but saw nothing of the witch she was now convinced she had dreamed up. Fortunately, Mrs Grisham's Ghost didn't reappear either. She secretly hoped Sheridan would visit soon; he was so much nicer than the other creatures she had encountered.

Mr Tempus kept Letisha entertained, offering her tasks if she had nothing to do, but also let her get on with her own business if she looked like she had something she would rather. On the third day, when she asked to go into the village just to get some fresh air, he was more than happy to let her. Mum would shriek at the idea of her doing anything alone, but Mr Tempus simply chuckled and recommended the local chip shop.

Covert Street was quiet and empty when Letisha returned, having stretched her legs and spent some of her pocket money. As two o'clock beckoned, the lunch break shoppers scuttled back to their offices, and the elderly ladies that nosed in the charity shop window moved towards the café for afternoon tea. Mr Tempus sat in the window working as usual, even as he nibbled the crust of a thin ham sandwich. He waved as she realised she was staring.
A ticking sound made Letisha feel as though she was already inside the shop. It was subtle at first, but as it grew slightly louder it sounded less like ticking and more like a swarm of insects. With her skin prickling at the prospect of being stung, Letisha spied the inky shadow of a man, lurking in the entry at the side of the shop. It lay between Mr Tempus's flat and the empty building next door. It had a for sale sign on it that was clearly ancient. He was tall and very thin, but moved too quickly for her to take in anything else. Letisha didn't hear him snigger to himself.

Mr Tempus greeted Letisha with a smile as she entered and put on the apron he had given her. It had become dirtied with just a few small smears of oil and a spot of blood from a paper cut, but finally it looked used and loved. Letisha liked that; it made her feel like she was doing something with herself.
       "Rain in the sky again," said Mr Tempus, holding a tiny screwdriver between his teeth. "Did anything keep you in town?"

Letisha sat on her stool, embarrassed. She realised that he was subtly implying that she was once again late. She had promised to be back by half one, and reminded herself that she must make more of an effort.

She struggled to see what he was doing as his task was so tiny. His long fingers flitted around the screwdriver so speedily it baffled the imagination. Finally, he slammed down his screwdriver and let out the breath he had been holding. He held up the small silver pocket watch that dangled on its chain proudly. It shone like glass, reflecting the numerous lamplights.

"I brought you an egg custard," she said, responding to his question at last, breaking the silence and dropping a paper bag on the counter.

"My favourite. How did you know?"

"Lucky guess?"

Mr Tempus nodded and took up the paper bag, as Letisha said,

"I saw a man,"

"Oh?" He said, uninterested, still admiring his work as he prepared to eat his custard. "Too few people appreciate a good watch nowadays."

"I saw a man in the entry," she repeated herself. "A thin, shadowy man. I think he was wearing a top hat. And I think you might have a wasps nest in the gutter or something…""

At that, Mr Tempus stopped and looked at her with narrowed eyes. "You didn't speak to him, did you?"

"No, he disappeared before I had a chance, as if he just melted into the shadows."

As she spoke, there came a rapping from the stock room door. It was not deep and booming like Sheridan's knocking, but short and impatient, made by thin knuckles.

Mr Tempus lowered his voice. "I know this chap. You must not speak to him unless he speaks to you first. Do you understand?"

"Okay…why?"

Mr Tempus paused to choose his words. "He's a little unconventional, a bit irrational at times. Here," he sat her at the workbench and handed her a cloth. "Polish the grease off those screwdrivers for me." Letisha took up her task, which was pointless as all the tools were spotless. She dropped the first screwdriver twice as she tried to stay calm.

Mr Tempus leaned in to whisper. "Keep your head down."

With that he disappeared into the stockroom to open the door. Trying not to let her anxiety overcome her, Letisha polished the screwdrivers with intent while trying to eavesdrop on the back room. Her shaking hands rattled the screwdriver against the worktop, echoing the rapping on the back door.

"Ah, come in, come in!" Mr Tempus exclaimed, and then there was some muttering. Letisha couldn't quite make out another voice, but Mr Tempus seemed nervous and uncomfortable, not his usual self at all. "Oh, no, she's just doing some cleaning for me, no need to check in…"

But it was too late. Out of the corner of her eye, she saw the little red curtain fly to one side. A tall thin man in a tall thin top hat marched through. He towered over Mr Tempus and narrowly avoided knocking his hat off in the low shop.

"Ah, here she is!" the visitor exclaimed, sweeping off his dented top hat and spreading his arms. His voice was like honey and his chocolate-coloured eyes gleamed. "Fancy trying to keep such a little gem a secret, Peter!"

Letisha receded just a little, taken back by his enthusiasm.

"I see my reputation does not precede me." He made a short bow. "Horatio Dreamseller, seller of the finest dreams, lotions and potions, at your service." He took her hand in his long bony fingers and shook it firmly. He wore navy blue fingerless gloves that had multiple repairs to them. As grandly Mr Dreamseller introduced himself, might have been mistaken for a tramp. Letisha realised she was staring.

"And your name is?" he asked expectantly.

"Letisha Tate," she managed.

"Always late, I presume. Your reputation precedes you. Do you like it here, Letisha?"

"Yes," she said. Behind Mr Dreamseller, Mr Tempus anxiously wrung his hands in his apron, as though he relied solely on Letisha to make a good impression

"Did you hear that, Peter? She likes it!"

Letisha blushed. She was still having trouble judging which side of the door he had emerged from. He was more frightening than Sheridan simply because of his gusto. He effortlessly made Mr Tempus uncomfortable when an eight-foot dragon seemed perfectly normal and was greeted as a friend. Still, there was something likeable about Mr Dreamseller. She felt herself slipping under his spell.

Mr Tempus didn't seem to appreciate his charms. As if he were summoning his last breath, he stuttered,

"How can we help you today, Mr Dreamseller?"

"I wanted to see how our new friend was getting on. We wouldn't want any mishaps, now would we?" He chuckled.

Mr Tempus shook his head, and seemed to be waiting for Mr Dreamseller to continue.

"I assume," said Dreamseller, "That Letisha has been introduced to the back door?"

"Of course."

"We had a visitor already…" Letisha began, but stopped as Mr Tempus nudged her, reiterating his warning of 'speak when you're spoken to.' Letisha bit her tongue and felt a foolish twinge in the pit of her stomach.

Mr Dreamseller smiled slyly and knelt down. With his long legs, he was just about the same height as Letisha on his knees. His trousers, corduroy striped in a dozen shades of red, were patched and threadbare.

"What a lovely girl you are," he said, lifting her chin with his hand. "With a mind of your own, too; a dangerous thing in a female. Wouldn't you agree, Mr Tempus?"

"Indeed," said Mr Tempus quietly.

"Tell me, Letisha, can I interest you in any dreams today?" asked Dreamseller.

"Pardon?" she stammered.

Mr Tempus was barely managing to contain his discomfort. He looked as though he might comically leap through the front window and run off into the afternoon at any second. Letisha hoped he could keep his cool.

"I," said Dreamseller grandly, "Am a seller of dreams, and the very best at that." He opened his scrappy green coat and revealed row after row of glass bottles, filled with a glittering substance in a rainbow of colours, some of which Letisha was not sure she could name. A squat bottle filled with a violet smoke that appeared to melt into liquid then turn back to smoke, caught Letisha's eye. Mr Dreamseller noticed immediately.

He took it out and held it up to her.

"This one?"

"I…I like the colour," she admitted.

"A good eye!" he exclaimed. "What a girl! This, my dear, is what we in the business call 'Waking Dream'. It is a good strong potion that encourages the most vivid and inspiring dreams! I have sold this to artists and poets across the land!"

"Oh," Letisha said, taking the bottle.

"Would you like it?"

"Um…" she began, hoping he wouldn't detect a lie. "I don't have any money, I'm sorry."

"A gift!" he exclaimed. "For you, my dear."

"Thank you," Letisha replied quietly, examining the bottle. "Um… what do I do with it?"

"Be careful," Mr Tempus blurted. "That bottle is not of this world, Letisha. But…Mr Dreamseller will tell you what to do."

"Indeed I will," snapped Mr Dreamseller, slitting his eyes momentarily at Mr Tempus, before turning back to Letisha and softening his tone. "All you do is simply take a little swig before bed, only a drop, mind, and it will taste of whatever you want it to."

"That's clever," she commented thoughtfully.

"A little trick I added myself." Mr Dreamseller straightened up. "Well then, since I see that everything is satisfactory, I'll be off. Mr Tempus, may I speak with you privately please?"

Letisha waited patiently in the shop, hoping that nobody would come in while she was alone. As she twiddled the bottle in her fingers, she couldn't seem to stop her hands shaking. She only wished Mr Tempus had warned her in more detail about Mr Dreamseller so she might have prepared herself a little better. Still, he didn't seem dangerous. Weird and unkempt, but not dangerous.

Mr Tempus re-entered looking tired and deflated.

"Well done," he said.

"Pardon?"

"I wasn't sure how you would cope; Mr Dreamseller doesn't always like children."

"He wasn't a dragon or a ghost," Letisha shrugged.

"That bottle he gave you, where is it?"

Letisha handed it over, where he checked it with a small magnifying glass. "You chose well. Some of the things he sells aren't nice, but you chose a good one. I don't recommend you use this though. Just admire it instead; it is a pretty colour, isn't it?"

"You can't possibly sell a dream," Letisha said. "Even I know that."

"Not in this world. The Otherworld is quite different. What you have there is liquid inspiration, a muse in a bottle if you will."

Letisha thought for a moment. "I don't have to tell my parents about this, do I?"

"I wouldn't recommend it," Mr Tempus smiled. "Anymore than I recommend telling them about Sheridan."

"It's best if you take care of it, I might drop it."

"Oh I wouldn't worry about that, Letisha," said Mr Tempus, and quite casually dropped the little bottle to the floor. She shrieked, expecting a smash. The dream hit the floor with a 'clink' and stood up by itself, as though there were a weight at its base. Letisha's jaw dropped.

"Otherworld Glass." Mr Tempus explained. "Near enough indestructible. I use it for my watch faces."

"Oh." Letisha said, retrieving the bottle and handing it to him.

"I'll put this out of sight; we wouldn't want Mr Dreamseller to be offended," said Mr Tempus cautiously. "And Letisha, thanks for the egg custard. I know your heart is in the right place, but you really must try not to get distracted in town."

"I know," she said, "I wasn't trying to sweeten you up."

"You were merely being kind," he smiled. "And it is most appreciated."

*

Mr Tempus allowed Letisha to bring her Waking Dream upstairs simply to look at, with the promise that she would not give in to its temptations. She had hoped he might let her use it to alleviate her boredom later on.
Letisha expected he was happy to have somebody to cook for again, as he was a simply marvellous chef. He made everything from scratch; pastry, soup and cakes among other things were all presented for her enjoyment. Stews, roast dinners, sausage and mash, cheese pie and quite simply the best gravy she had ever had. What did baffle her was how old-fashioned his tastes were; there was no pasta or curry, or even any tinned food. She went to bed every evening with a full belly, and felt slightly guilty for yearning for pasta shapes in tomato sauce, or microwave chips. Her parents didn't spend much time cooking so watching Mr Tempus was a real education.

"So if I did use this in the Otherworld," she said, holding up the Waking Dream and looking at Mr Tempus through the purple substance. "What would happen?"

Mr Tempus shrugged, as he placed an enormous pasty and a mountain of real chips in front of her. "'Not sure. But I wouldn't test it."

"Has he ever given you anything?" she asked. A puff of steam escaped the pasty as she stuck in her fork, warming her cheeks

"Only the creeps," Mr Tempus chuckled, before looking around as if restlessly somebody might have heard him.
She blew on a particularity monstrous chip. "Why are you so afraid of him? I thought he seemed nice."

Mr Tempus stopped chewing and swallowed. "It's complicated."

"Oh. Because I thought maybe you owed him money or something. My Dad is always going on about loan sharks and what horrible people they are."

"No, it's not like that," Mr Tempus smiled. She wanted him to see that she cared. "It's nothing you need to worry yourself with."

"Oh," she said, and they continued eating in silence. Once again she felt as if she had been cheated out of the truth.

Letisha treated herself to a bath after tea. The bathroom was tiny, tiled floor to ceiling in shining dark green tiles. It had a luxurious freestanding bath, much fancier than what she was used to at home.

She had left Mr Tempus working on a crossword, feeling like she needed an early night after all the worry of Mr Dreamseller. She didn't like seeing Mr Tempus so distressed. It just didn't seem fair.

She tidied the bathroom when she was finished before returning to her room. Mr Tempus had kindly made up the fire, though it did little to combat the cold. The flames sent shadows dancing around her as she began the lengthy task of combing her hair. It was no easy task; when straight it fell well past her waist and each curl needed to be conditioned and combed, lest she look like she'd been dragged through a hedge the next morning. She tried to avoid looking at the initials in the mirror, fearing her eyes might play tricks on her. Or worse, a ghost might actually appear. She wasn't beyond believing it could happen.

The house was quiet beyond the whispering of the fire. Only the distant roar of traffic drifted down the street, from the road that connected the backwater town to the rest of the world. Despite the stay getting easier, Letisha still longed to be on that road heading home, where she had her own room with a television and books she liked.

She called goodnight to Mr Tempus, who was still reading the paper where she had left him. He called back and watched her disappear into her room, before going back to a crossword he had no intention of finishing.

8

FATHER TIME HIMSELF

It was past midnight, and still the ticking from the clocks drifted on the air louder than ever. Letisha questioned how she had ever managed to sleep through it before. She had laid awake for what felt like hours, thinking about ghosts and all manner of things that might drift out of her imagination. The dying fire turned every shadow into a goblin, every movement from the trees outside a giant. Her fantasies would not be so fuelled by a pitch-black room, she thought.

Unable to stand it any more, Letisha got out of bed and opened the door. The noise became louder on the landing. The kitchenette and living area were dark and empty, but a green light seeping from beneath a door to her right caught her attention. She could hear Mr Tempus muttering to himself. Was he still working downstairs?

Letisha crept towards the end of the landing, to a door unlike the others. It looked much older, with splintered panels and flaking paint, peeling even as she stared. The door was growing older before her eyes.

Letisha cleared her throat. "Mr Tempus?"

No answer came, just the relentless ticking. Letisha repeated herself a fraction louder and knocked. She feared turning the knob would force it to fall to pieces.

Letisha jumped back as there came a glimmer of white dust, which sprung from the very cracks of the old door. In a second it was restored like new. The little brass doorknob shone. Letisha felt her tired eyes grow wide in surprise, as the wood appeared to begin to paint itself a rich glossy green.

When the new door was finished, the ticking stopped, and the house was silent. Letisha held her breath, as time appeared to be standing still. In the absence of the clocks' voices, she called out again.

"Mr Tempus?" She heard him shuffling. "I heard some noise."

Mr Tempus sighed. "I suppose you'd better come in before the lock starts to stick again."

The green door opened, smooth as silk. Letisha was almost as tall as Mr Tempus anyway, but he seemed more hunched than usual as he met her. He wore long dark red robes and a hat that drooped down his back. The robes were embellished with a fine silver thread, and the pockets were overflowing with cogs and wheels and all other manner of the clock parts she recognized from downstairs.

Mr Tempus did not look shocked to see her. His eyes were glazed, as if he were working without really paying attention.

"I thought you were asleep." He yawned and stroked his beard.

She jumped as there came a loud chime from inside the room and then, as if the first had counted all the others in, a great number of clocks began to tick, chime and clang, as if each was competing to be the loudest.

"Excuse me for a moment," Mr Tempus turned into the room. He then bellowed, "Quiet!" The room fell guiltily silent. "They're excited."

"I'm sorry?" Letisha asked, confused. "Who's excited?"

"The clocks," he explained, opening the door so she could see inside. "It's been a long time since they saw anyone but me."

The clocks began to tick enthusiastically, their song echoing off the high walls in a metallic chorus. Every wall was lined with metal racks, as well as hundreds more in between them. It was like a great library full with noisy clocks of all sizes and colours. Letisha realised that Mr Tempus also held a clock in his hand; a small old fashioned alarm clock, with two flat round bells like a mouse's ears on its top, and a blue face with a sun and moon painted on in exquisite golden detail. The clock wriggled in his hands like an animal.

"Miss Suzanne Allbritten, a Spiritualist from Stoke on Trent," he explained.

Letisha was confused. "She's a customer?"

"Of sorts. I haven't touched her clock for a long time but she's just had an operation that will put years on her life, so I'm giving it a tweak. A very lucky lady."

Letisha frowned, looking in disbelief at the strange room that was somehow squeezed into what could only be a broom cupboard in ordinary circumstances. Beside a desk in the middle of the shelving system sat a pile of clocks in a box simply tabled 'IN', and on the desk itself sat a tray of tools, antique versions of the ones used downstairs. Mr Tempus kept his tools in excellent condition, but these looked tired and well worn.

For the first time she took in how high the ceiling was. They were upstairs already, and it was impossibly far about them. The room, easily as vast as her school hall, had tall narrow windows placed at intervals showing the clear night outside.

Mr Tempus was tinkering with the back of Miss Allbritten's squirming clock. Letisha struggled to make words.

"Mr Tempus, I get the feeling I'm standing on the edge of another Portal."

"Well, I haven't a clue why," he said without taking his eyes off his work. "This is no Portal, this is my Watch Room."

"Your collection?"

"My burden," he said flatly. "You should go back to bed."

"I'm not tired," she lied, stifling a yawn. She was desperate for him to explain himself, but he seemed only to want to tinker with the giggling clock. She had barely managed a wink of sleep because of the noise, and now there was this to keep her awake as well. "Please, what is all this about?"

Suddenly, the clock jumped and righted itself. It ticked a little faster, and then slowed to a comfortable, more natural resting beat. Mr Tempus looked at her over his little glasses

"Curiosity killed the cat," he said darkly.

"I'm not a cat," she replied. She wasn't nearly as sure-footed as a cat, and certainly didn't have nine lives.

Mr Tempus eyed her suspiciously. "Sometimes, you remind me of my son. He never knew when to stop asking questions either. There are things in this room, my dear, which will send your eyeballs spinning in their sockets. Make you question everything you ever thought you knew. And things," he added sorrowfully, "That will scare you away from this place forever."

Letisha reached out and took Miss Allbritton's clock, cradling it gently, and looked the old man in the eye. "You don't scare me, Mr Tempus. You're a kind man."

"But Father Time is not. Were the orders given I would have to stop this clock, and end the life of an innocent woman. But that is life, dictated by the hand of Time, as cruel and unpredictable as the sea, and as vast as the atoms of the universe."

Letisha began to feel frightened. She had never heard Mr Tempus talk like that before, worried at what she had unwittingly disturbed. As poetic as his words were, she was not sure she understood them. She felt very young and stupid.

She narrowed her eyes. "Who are you?"

"I am fond of you, so I'm not sure how much of the truth I can really tell you. This is so much bigger than dragons and dreamsellers."

"I'm good at keeping secrets," she said, mimicking what he had said to her when encouraging her to share her dream. She had still made no mention of Selena, despite bursting to blab.

"Is that so? Why should I believe you?"

"Anyone I told would just call me a liar and insist I stop making up silly stories. They wouldn't believe your story in a million years." Letisha folded her arms; she was being completely honest.

"Yet you would?"

"If you'd trust me."

Mr Tempus sighed and ran a hand over his beard. "A long time ago," he said, "I was Peter Tempus, and by day I still am. But for now, I must serve my sentence as Father Time, governing all the time in the world, until I am released from my burden."

Letisha shook her head in disbelief. "So all these clocks, these are peoples' lives?"

"In a manner of speaking. Your time keeping is terrible but you really are a clever girl, Letisha." She decided he was trying to distract her with compliments.

"So do I have a clock in here?"

"Somewhere," he said. Letisha noticed him begin to edge out of the room, further blocking her view. "But I've never had to do anything with it so I can't tell you where it is off the top of my head."

He glanced at a small watch on his wrist; it was much less lively than the one belonging to the spiritualist.

"You really ought to go back to bed. Your parents won't forgive me for keeping you up late with all this nonsense."

"But…"

"Not another word. All will be explained, if you will just go back to bed and leave me to finish my work for the evening. Can you do that for me?"

She nodded. "Only if you promise."

"I promise. Now off you pop, and it won't be long before I turn in myself."

*

With Letisha finally in bed and the clocks settling down, Mr Tempus returned to his work

He decided to look for the clock belonging to Letisha Tate. A younger clock would be in the racks at the back of the room, so he shuffled along the way, carefully replacing Miss Allbritton's clock on his route. It settled snugly into its place and prepared to rest; like its owner, its ordeal was over.

The racks not only sat almost twenty feet above them, but also twenty feet below the suspended floor, falling into an vast system of oily cogs and gears. Mr Tempus had designed the intricate scheme to keep his clocks organised.

He was tremendously proud of it, even if it did represent his nightly hindrance.

Mr Tempus flicked a switch, and the groaning of clockwork and ingenious engineering made the rack jolt and shift, rotating shelf after shelf before him, before he stopped without looking up. After searching for only a second, he came to the item he was looking for. Letisha's clock was a vibrant shade of purple, with silver bells atop its body, and a yellow face with blue spots and pink numbers. Below the '12' where a makers' seal would normally fall was inscribed the name 'L. Tate'. Her date of birth was inscribed below but so far nothing else of any importance had been recorded. Letisha's clock suited her absolutely; mismatched but charming. It doddered about like a fat old cat woken from a heavy slumber.

Mr Tempus carried the colourful timepiece back to his workbench and sat down with it in front of him. It leaned back on its rim, staring blankly. Mr Tempus didn't like handling younger clocks, as he knew most commonly only heartache was to be found

"Well then, Miss Tate," he picked up a screwdriver. "Let's see what we can do about your timekeeping skills."

9

THE DREADED STACKHOUSE

Letisha awoke the next morning at half seven sharp. She hadn't even set an alarm the night before.

She dressed leisurely and tidied her hair. She even had time to ponder over the letters T.T., still present on the mirror despite her efforts to rub them off. She considered showing the ghostly monogram to Mr Tempus, but quickly decided against it, since he had enough on his plate.

Within half an hour she was sitting at the table enjoying a slice of buttered granary toast with Mr Tempus. He paid little attention to her early rising. He only seemed happy to have company for breakfast.

At half eight, the washing up done and a few items prepared ready for tea, they left the kitchenette and descended to the shop. It was still dark with the blinds drawn, despite a little morning light trying to work its way in through the gaps.

Mr Tempus had Letisha carry the little A-board advertising his services out onto the high street, and as she returned he was just pulling up the blinds and dusting the window. The sign on the door still said 'Closed' as she peered through the leaded glass to watch him work. She had given no thought to what had occurred the night before, convinced that she had once again drifted into the ever vivid realm of her imagination.

Letisha watched Mr Tempus put out the display in the window, which he had done every morning well before she was awake. They dusted all the clocks on the walls, polished the work surfaces, and cleaned tools if needed.

She went to work on the wall display with a duster made from ostrich feathers, but found barely a speck of dust in the entire shop. As Mr Tempus turned the 'Closed' sign to 'Open', Letisha took her place behind the counter. She could contain her questions no longer.

"Is it very difficult to keep all those clocks upstairs as clean as this?"

Mr Tempus stopped vigorously polishing a small silver spanner and contemplated her question. "I can't imagine what you mean."

He looked up at her, and took something that was stuck in her hair. He held up a dandelion seed.

"Dandelion clocks were Toby's favourite," he smiled, examining the little seed in his fingers.

Letisha cocked her eyebrow, and began to question if anything had happened in The Watch Room the previous evening.

"You told me that you carried a heavy burden, and that every person has a clock. You gave a lady named Suzanne something more time because she'd had an operation. There was a room, with racks and racks of clocks in all colours, and you wore a funny hat. There was a door that aged, and then was like new again. You said...you said Father Time is not a kind man." Mr Tempus was silent, still polishing the spanner very slowly, though it shone already. Letisha felt as though she had embarrassed him, as he put down the spanner, lined it up perfectly with the edge of the worktop. He knitted his fingers in his lap and looked at her seriously.

"You haven't been at that Waking Dream in the night, have you?" Letisha felt a pang of insecurity in the pit of her stomach. He had said himself that the old house could lend itself to the imagination. Perhaps the place was merely giving her ideas. Her defence was interrupted by the bell above the door. An old lady entered and Mr Tempus jumped enthusiastically to her service. Letisha continued to polish the tools just for something to do. She was only really used for fetching things from the back when there was a customer in the shop, so she tried to make herself scarce.

The lady was only after a new battery, and Mr Tempus had replaced it within seconds. The customer was thanking him and on her way out only a moment later.

When they were alone again, Mr Tempus finally spoke.

"Oh, I got a phone call from your Aunt Stackhouse; she's coming today."

"Why didn't you tell me?" Letisha cried.

"I didn't want to worry you. Don't tell me you wouldn't have laid awake worrying about her if you'd known about it."

"Oh," Letisha said shortly. She was slightly irritated that he had dismissed the previous evening as if she were making it up.

"Don't worry, I'm not going to give you a bad report. And moreover," he lowered his voice as a figure passed the window. "We don't talk about the Watch Room outside the Watch Room." With that he put away the little box of batteries, and knitted his fingers together as the door opened, and an all too familiar woman entered the shop. Immediately, the very sight of Aunt Stackhouse struck fear into Letisha's heart as she began to feel guilty for something she hadn't done. She had heard that Aunt Stackhouse had that effect on most of her pupils when she was teaching.

"Hello, Peter." She hissed. "And hello, Letisha."

"Hello, Aunt Liz," said Letisha quietly, and decided keeping busy was a good idea. She knew Aunt Stackhouse wasn't here to check up on her, really, but only to make sure that Mr Tempus was doing such an awful job that next time she would get Letisha instead. Why on earth she would want to offer hospitality to somebody she couldn't stand was a mystery.

Secretly Letisha prayed that Sheridan would burst through the back door and send Aunt Stackhouse shrieking into the morning. Just the thought of it forced her to repress a chuckle. Still, she hoped she could get through the visit without being made to cry.

Aunt Stackhouse had the cold green eyes of a skinny underfed tiger, ready to pounce on any bit of meat lying around. She always wore the same brown cardigan that hung from her skinny frame as if from a washing line. Her plaid skirt didn't match. She was truly set in her ways, and felt threatened by anyone different or even a little bit colourful. It was no surprise that Letisha's aunt hated her own free-spiritedness with a passion.

"So," said Aunt Stackhouse, grinning like a cat with a bowl of cream. "How is she behaving? I trust you have become acquainted with Letisha's special brand of chaos. I told her parents I would make sure she wasn't running rings round you or wasting any of your precious time."

Mr Tempus looked over at Letisha, then back at her aunt. "Actually, Liz, I have found she is kind and very helpful. All the customers love her. I'd say she has been nothing short of a little star. I am considering asking her back on Saturdays when she's a little older. We were discussing the matter just as you arrived, weren't we, Letisha?"

Letisha almost choked, and then felt guilty knowing that she and Mr Tempus really did get on well. "Yes, Mr Tempus," she managed at last.

Aunt Stackhouse was speechless, but not for long. "But you haven't found that she is clumsy, or lazy?"

"Not in the least. She's a dab-hand with a screwdriver."

Aunt Stackhouse turned slightly red across the nose, and ran a purple tongue over dry lips. No doubt she had been looking forward to giving Letisha a good telling off and relaying the news to her parents, but Mr Tempus wasn't playing along. He stood his ground firmly while remaining ever pleasant and accommodating. This made Aunt Stackhouse very cross.

"Well," she muttered, leaning in closer to Letisha. "Let's hope you haven't just convinced Mr Tempus to lie on your behalf. Hmm?"

"Yes, Aunt Liz." Letisha chirped quietly.

"Well, I must be going. Lots of work to be done to make sure the new term gets off without a hitch. I'm especially looking forward to grading your homework, Letisha." Aunt Stackhouse leered. Letisha was awful at maths, no matter how hard she tried, and did not expect her aunt to be sympathetic.

With that, Stackhouse turned sharply on her flat black heel and exited, slamming the door behind her. Her mood was so icy that the little bell was afraid to jingle. When she was out of earshot, Mr Tempus said.

"Well, she hasn't changed at all."

Letisha had gone back to polishing the tools, and she simply shook her head in response to his statement.

"Don't worry. She might drop in to check in on you, but I'm the one who's in charge. Now, I believe there is the question of our little discussion, which your delightful aunt interrupted."

10

WHAT HAPPENS IN THE WATCH ROOM

"What happens in the Watch Room stays in the Watch Room," Mr Tempus finished at the top of the stairs, pulling a key from his pocket and turning it in the brass doorknob. The door had long since aged again, and the paint flaked away as Mr Tempus pushed against the wood. It stuck momentarily, before relenting with a creak. Inside, he flicked an ancient switch and the lights blinked to life with several successive bangs. Once again the racks were illuminated as they had been the night before.

"I knew I wasn't dreaming." Letisha whispered.

"Of course you weren't," said Mr Tempus. "But do you really think I can expose this lot to just anyone?"

"I guess you can't," Letisha agreed, gazing up and realising the windows above now showed daylight outside. It was lunchtime, but before they ate Mr Tempus had suggested they take another look. She turned to him. "What is this place, really?"

"Time, my dear, Time itself. Exactly like you learned last night, for every single person in the world, there is a timepiece, which is stored in this room. And this," he said, picking up a purple clock with silver bells, "Is yours."

He handed it to her, and she held it carefully. It jumped up and down and wagged its back end like a little dog.

"This can't possibly be mine," she pointed at the clock on the wall. "It's running on time."

"Actually, I think you'll find it's now ten minutes fast. I dug it out and gave it a tweak last night. As it turns out, your problem with time was simply a slow movement. From now on you'll have little trouble with getting anywhere on time.

"It's got my birthday on it," she remarked, turning it over despite the clock's protestations.

"Oh yes, everyone's clock has that. Our clocks are the trackers for the events in our lives that define who we are; Miss Allbritton's clock now has a record of the day her life began anew. You are so young nothing major has been recorded as yet. But don't worry, it will."

"All this thing does is keep my time?"

"Yes, but it is also your life; every cog and gear moves in motion as you move. Time is the currency of the universe and it affects all of us in the same way. As you travel through your life, you affect the gears of other people's clocks, on your mother's and father's, for example. I don't doubt your birth is recorded on both of theirs."

"When will something be added to my clock?"

"When an event occurs that will change the direction of your life."

"Oh..." she said, handing the little clock back as she tried to make sense of things. "Well, thank you. I'm not sure how you did it, though."

"All in a day's work for Father Time. Now, I'm sure we have already established that this, just like the Portal," He tapped his nose. "This is our little secret. I'm sure Aunt Stackhouse would find some way to turn this against us if she found out, wouldn't you agree?"

Mr Tempus locked up the Watch Room, and they made their way to the kitchen. They ate a short meal of crumpets and jam, and he allowed Letisha to ask more questions about his secret room.

"So how does it work? That space should only be as big as a broom cupboard, surely."

"On the same principle as everything else on the other side of the Portal: Magic."

"Oh. And how did you get a job as Father Time? Surely you can't be the only one?"

"I am, I'm afraid," he sighed, spreading more jam on his second crumpet. Letisha noticed the label on the jar stated that it was 'A gift from the kitchen of Sheridan and Sigmund'.

"Does Sheridan know that you are Father Time?" She asked, examining the jar.

"No, my dear, he doesn't. Can you imagine how he would react if he saw a room that size filled with clocks?"

Letisha felt frustrated, as he seemed slow to give her any real details. The secret was out, so it seemed only fair that he should tell her the whole truth. So far squeezing it out of him was proving difficult. As if he read her mind, Mr Tempus said,

"This is a burden, Letisha. A long time ago, I vowed to take the job as Father Time so that my son might be spared. He was very sick. He stands suspended in time, until my sentence is done and the original Father Time returns to his duty, and I can hopefully get my son treated for his illness..."

"So your son is alive!" she cried, though she felt no less uncomfortable for knowing it. "I thought you said everything here works with magic. Can't you cure sickness with magic?"

Mr Tempus solemnly shook his head. "Not on this side of the Portal, or on the other. Nature is funny like that. We are mortal for a reason. His illness would be no problem now, a simple trip to the hospital. But it wasn't always like that."

Letisha was unsure if she understood. She desperately wanted to know more about his son. She wondered just how long he had been serving this sentence as guardian of the Watch Room.

"Mr Tempus, how old are you?"

"Oh, I forget exactly. Let's see, I must be coming up for at least one hundred and forty or so.. My birthday is in April, but I've seen so many Aprils and I've become accustomed to having nobody to celebrate or share a birthday with. I had a wife and a son once, but this job is one that must be done alone…"

"Well, you have me now, don't you?"

"Ah yes," he perked up suddenly. "And I have a gift for you…"

"What is it?"

Mr Tempus reached over to the kitchen counter, taking up an ancient book. It was gloriously old and dog-eared.

"Classic Time-Pieces and Collectibles," Letisha read the title. "Why are you giving it to me?"

"To bind our friendship," he told her "So you must treasure it always."

*

On Friday afternoon, Sheridan dropped in for a visit to see how Letisha was getting along. As they sat in the back room looking through Letisha's new book together, Mr Tempus tidied up the shop for the night. He had brought a tray of tea and biscuits down for them to share.

Sheridan, who proudly showed off his polished horns, delighted in pointing out items he owned that were shown in the book.

"Ah, this one," he said, pointing to an enamel faced creation, "is an Irish Verge Pocket Watch. That's real Silver, you know. Made in 1821, with a Paircase movement! I don't have one yet but I'm counting on Mr Tempus to find one for me!"

Mr Tempus chuckled slightly, hearing their conversation through the curtain. Sheridan sipped his tea noisily from the cup much too small for his enormous clawed hand, though he held up his little finger as manners dictated. He nibbled on a shortbread biscuit from his other hand.

"Turn the page, let's see the next one!" His lisp was all the more prominent in his excitement.

Letisha turned the page to come face to face with a very ordinary looking watch. It had a gold case with a simple delicate swirl engraved into it, and three crystals set into the design, one green, one blue, and one red. The image had been printed onto semi-transparent paper, as had the next two leaves. Letisha turned away from the watch's case, to its face, which was again, really quite ordinary, until Sheridan pointed out one unusual thing;

"Look at that; no makers' seal," he jabbed one clawed finger. "There's more!"

Letisha turned the next leaf, to be met with what the author had described as 'The Second Face'. In its centre was a small vial of green liquid, not dissimilar to the bottles carried by Mr Dreamseller. Eight cogs, labelled by the author as 'controls', each claiming a different effect on Time itself, surrounded the vial.

Sheridan was practically dribbling over the discovery. Letisha turned back to read the name of the watch, which she struggled to pronounce;

"Ouro…bor…ros…" she managed nervously.

"Ouroboros." Sheridan said more confidently. "I think I've seen this somewhere before."

Letisha turned to the Third Face, which was laden with six 'Pawn Cogs' and one 'Master Cog' at the centre of it all. She read the description aloud:

"'One individual can be controlled with all the actions on the Second Face. Each cog can affect the others, as well as the Master Cog. It reminds us of how our own actions and the actions of those around us have consequences, linking us as delicately as the movements of the clock itself.'"

Letisha smiled, reminded of how Mr Tempus had explained that her own actions would affect the actions of others. He had indeed read the book from cover to cover many times.

"It's a bit philosophical for a reference book, if you don't mind my saying so," Sheridan remarked.

The cuckoo clock signalled that it was time to close. Letisha stood with the book still open. It weighed a ton in her arms.

"You know, I'm sure I have a watch like that, somewhere." Sheridan scratched his beard as he tried to remember. "It doesn't look like much, and I've never seen the other faces, but the case is certainly familiar."

Mr Tempus pushed aside the curtain. "Most people now believe the Ouroboros to be purely fictional, Sheridan; the stuff of myth."

"If I might be so bold," Sheridan pointed out, "Dragons are also believed to be the 'stuff of myth'."

"You've got a point," Mr Tempus agreed thoughtfully. "Still, I imagine I could retire on what one of those things would cost, wouldn't you say?"

"Fourteen down," Mr Tempus said, tapping the pencil on his lip as he surveyed the crossword. "White as a ghost. Five letters."
They had retired to the lounge after dinner, full of steak and kidney pie. Doing her best to put Aunt Stackhouse out of her mind, Letisha had spent some time looking at her new book. As her eyes grew tired she resorted to watching the television, but much to her disappointment there was nothing to watch. Mr Tempus did not have cable, though he hardly watched television anyway. Even so, she was distracted and failed to answer his question.

"So I can't ask about the Watch Room," she said, suddenly bored of the television.

"Nope."

"But can I ask about the back door?"

"You know there's not much I can tell you."

"Well that's good, because I'm not even sure what to ask. How can two places be the same place at once?"

"You're asking about you-know-where, aren't you?" he almost sang at her.

"Not exactly. When Sheridan is on the porch at the back at the shop, how is it that if I was to stand in the alley in this world that I wouldn't see him? And don't just say its 'magic' because what my dad does is magic and I can see straight through it!"
Mr Tempus pressed his fingers together in a pyramid, trying to form a response that would satisfy her. He took up the empty biscuit packet beside him, opened it out flat, and took a moment to blow the crumbs off his lap. He then laid the clear plastic out on top of his newspaper.

"The newspaper is where we are," he said. Letisha cocked her head on one side. "You have to use your imagination, Letisha."

"Fine," she rolled her eyes. "The newspaper is us."

"And the biscuit packet is somewhere else."

"What?"

"The newspaper is the solid, visible place. The biscuit packet is clear, and not always visible, even when it is the same place. The only way you can get to see the biscuit packet is if you know how."

"Is the biscuit packet the Watch Room?" she asked dumbly.

"You mentioned it again!" he cried, waving the packet around and pointing.
She knew he was only joking, but she still worried why he was so concerned about speaking about it when it was just the two of them in an empty house. Mr Tempus folded the packet away, and placed his newspaper on the table. "Do you understand?"

"I think so. I suppose turning the key in a certain way is our way of seeing the Otherworld and the Watch…biscuit packet."

"That's right. Only as I said before, you must promise not to go out into the Otherworld or into you-know-where without me," he reminded her firmly.

"I know," she nodded, yawning widely. She concluded that Mr Tempus's bizarre explanation had pushed her over the edge, and it was time for bed. She wasn't sure she understood his explanation, but she was closer than before.

11

DANGER

Letisha awoke early on morning Saturday. Eyeing the letters T.T on the mirror as she left her room, she found the hallway dark, and the kitchenette empty. She could not shake the air of discomfort that crept about her shoulders as she descended the stairs. Mr Tempus made no sound, either in the shop or the flat. The house was dark and eerily quiet. A howling gale shook the window panes.

As the wind died down she realised somebody was singing.
    "Tick-tock, tick-tock," sang a strangely familiar voice. Letisha reached the bottom of the staircase, and the song grew louder.
    "Tick-tock, tick-tock. I'm the best at collecting clocks."
Immediately his distinctive lisp gave him away. Letisha switched on the light to find Sheridan sitting amongst dozens of open boxes. One of the huge shelving units had been pulled down, scattering cogs, screws and other components all over the floor. A few tiles had cracked where it had fallen. Several tiles had even been dragged up, as if somebody had suspected treasures hidden beneath them. Even the old staircase had dents where debris had hit. Letisha dreaded how Mr Tempus would react if he saw his beloved shop in such a state.
Sheridan was wearing watches up both his arms, dangling from his chubby clawed feet, and stuffed into his pockets. He wore a ruined cuckoo clock on his head, his horns pushed through the little red roof.
    "Cuckoo, cuckoo, I've got more shiny watches than you!" He chirped with his snout through the cuckoo's doorway.
    "Sheridan?" Letisha whispered.
Sheridan froze before making a poor attempt at closing the little doors about his large horned nose. "Sheridan's not here," he muttered sheepishly.
Letisha tried to remain calm; she resolved that Mr Tempus was missing, and her only witness at hand was little more than a hare-brained, watch-thieving dragon.
    "Sheridan, where is Mr Tempus?"
    The dragon shuffled awkwardly. Summoning up all her courage Letisha reached up and opened the little doors. Yellow eyes peered out with a guilty look.

"Ah! Miss Tate! I let myself in as the door was open just a crack, and…" he paused to fabricate an excuse. "I fell into the shelves!"
She was lost for words.

"What do you think of my new hat?" he went on.

"It's very nice," she managed. Going along with his little prank might be the safest option. "Do you know where Mr Tempus is?"

"Haven't a clue," Sheridan replied, attempting to remove his 'hat'. It was well and truly wedged. He blushed. "Do you think perhaps you could…?"

"Oh, of course," Letisha said, and stood on her toes attempting to loosen the clock from the bottom. Even sitting, Sheridan was much taller than her and legs began to burn from standing on her tiptoes. "Perhaps we could take it apart."

Sheridan sat patiently while Letisha stood on her stool and dismantled the clock with a screwdriver from Mr Tempus's tool kit.
When it finally came free, Sheridan began removing the watches from his arms, guiltily replacing them in their boxes as best he could. Letisha attempted to clear some of the mess, though she had no hope of fixing the shelves.

Mr Tempus was nowhere to be found when she checked the shop. The front door was securely locked and no mess had been made. Curiously enough, the door was bolted from the inside.

"I'm so sorry about all this," Sheridan admitted tearfully. "I got over excited when I realised I was unsupervised amongst all the beautiful timepieces. I swear I only made some of the mess. I didn't knock over any of the units, and I certainly wouldn't throw anything valuable so carelessly around the place. I panicked when I couldn't find Mr Tempus… I did swing around and take a chunk out of the bannister, but other than that I was just playing with the things I picked up out of the mess!"

Letisha narrowed her eyes. Sheridan made no secret of his mania where timepieces were concerned. Mr Tempus said he didn't dare think about Sheridan in the Watch Room. But despite his clumsiness and his collecting, Sheridan showed nothing but the greatest respect for Mr Tempus.

Letisha decided to listen to her instincts. Sheridan was mad, but he was no liar. "So if you haven't seen Mr Tempus, where is he?"

"Perhaps he had an appointment," Sheridan suggested.

"He wouldn't just run off and leave me on my own," Letisha folded her arms at Sheridan's poor suggestion. "Look at this place; talk about a bull in a china shop."

"There's a bull in here?!" Sheridan shrieked, hopping onto his fat tiptoes and clutching his tail away from the floor.

Letisha shook her head. "It's a figure of speech, Sheridan. We have to approach this logically. While my parents are working, Mr Tempus is in charge of me. He wouldn't just go out and leave a mess like this, no matter what. He wouldn't leave me by myself without an explanation either. And he wouldn't..." she trailed off, realising that Sheridan shouldn't have been able to get in.

"He wouldn't what?"

"He wouldn't leave the back door open to the Otherworld. He's always talking about unsavoury characters wandering in."

"Now, wait just a minute!" Sheridan protested.

"Not you, silly. An unsavoury character who might do this. Not only that, the shop is locked from the inside."

Sheridan looked at her with wide, expectant eyes. Either he really was quite dim, or he was allowing her to come to her own conclusions.

"What if," he muttered, "Somebody took him?"

"You mean a kidnapper? But the shop is locked up; the only way anyone could get in is... " They both turned to look at the back door. "Somebody must have come in from your side."

"My side?" he gasped, affronted. "Why do you assume that?"

"Because who in this world breaks in and takes the jeweller instead of the jewels?"

For one fleeting moment Letisha considered calling the police. But then she tried to think how she would explain her story, not to mention why the only real witness was a dragon. The police would probably arrest her for wasting time, and then her parents would be furious, so something needed to be done. "Sheridan," she began slowly in what she would later conclude was a moment of madness. "Could you take me into your world?"

"Oh no, there are strict rules on that sort of thing, Miss Tate," said the dragon sternly.

"And what are they?" Letisha asked, sensing his bluff.

"Well," Sheridan tapped his temple and held his chin.

Letisha put her hands on her hips sternly. "If we don't find Mr Tempus, who's going to repair your watches and create new commissions for you?" She paused, before removing her own watch and offering it to him. "If you take me through, I'll give you this."

Sheridan's eyes lit up with glee. "Here's what you do; take the key." He pointed to the long dirty key hanging on a hook by the door. "And turn it clockwise in the lock. Then, turn it clockwise again and it will open into the Otherworld."

Silently, Letisha reached up and took the key, only to realise that the door was open. It made sense since there was no other way that Sheridan would have been able to enter. Mr Tempus always knew when the dragon was coming, and prepared accordingly.

"Was Mr Tempus expecting you this morning, Sheridan?" Letisha asked quietly, her nerves tingling as the truth became apparent.

"Well, no." Sheridan said. "I actually came to see you, to ask if I could take another look at your book. It might help me label some of my collection…"

"The door wasn't opened from the inside," Letisha concluded. "And if it was, then Mr Tempus let in whoever took him,"

"I see," Sheridan agreed, stroking his beard. "Well then, we'd better do some sleuthing, hadn't we?"

Letisha nodded. She did as she was told, only to find the door already open.

Sheridan shrugged. "Well, that's how I found it and I didn't want to lock myself in."

Letisha rolled her eyes. It took all her strength to pull the door to open. The handle was rough and stubborn in her hands, but eventually it yielded and a huge gust of cold wind blew leaves around her feet. She fell back into Sheridan's belly. Her hair was whipped back and her cheeks stung. A single brave candle inside a glass lantern lit the porch.

"What time is it?" Letisha asked, righting herself.

"Fifty seven minutes and forty two seconds past seven," reported Sheridan from his new watch.

"But it's still dark here."

"Oh yes," Sheridan agreed. "Winter is hard in Mule Root."

"I thought this was the Otherworld."

"It is. But this particular part is called Mule Root. Over there in the distance are the Blue Mountains, and just in front of them is Gram-Shank. You can see it all on a clear day."

*

Before they left she decided to check the Watch Room. Letisha was still hoping Mr Tempus would turn up and explain everything, but secretly she yearned to see the Otherworld. Sheridan didn't need to know the reason she was going back upstairs, so she followed up with a little white lie.

"I just want to make sure he hasn't left the iron on or anything," she lied. "We can't be sure nothing has been taken from down here can we?"

"It looks as if they were looking for something and got into a tantrum when they couldn't find it." Sheridan mused. "What were they after?"

"I can only imagine," she said, ascending the stairs. Perhaps Selena had come back and lost her patience, destroying the stockroom in a fit of frustration.

Letisha collected her hat and coat from her room, assuming she would need them for the journey. As she picked up her satchel, she looked at the letters on the mirror, still staring back at her and unchanging as ever.

"T.T." She sighed, as she was still unable to wipe them away. " I don't have time to worry about ghosts now. Whatever you are, you're going to have to wait."

Steeling herself, Letisha turned her attention to the Watch Room, lonely and dark at the end of the corridor. The door was old once more, but it was now unchanging. If Mr Tempus was hiding inside, he was doing an excellent job of keeping quiet.
She turned the key, and was surprised as she opened it into a small dark broom cupboard, barely big enough to stand in amongst the cleaning supplies.

"Oh, for goodness' sake," she sighed, feeling foolish. She stepped back and shut the door, before turning the key anti-clockwise once more. She hoped the mechanism would work much the same as the back door. Success! The door creaked open, and she stepped inside.

Letisha felt as though she were walking into a tomb. The high windows were laced with dusty cobwebs, as were the racks of clocks. Everything was covered in ancient brown dust. She sneezed, the sound echoing off the walls. Suddenly, a familiar face, or so to speak, appeared from out of the shadows; a face with twelve numbers, three hands, and two silver bells that jingled with joy to see her. Letisha's clock joyfully wiggled its way over to her.

"What's happened here, clock?" she asked.
She picked it up, where it trembled in her hands. Letisha felt dread spike in her chest. It seemed nowhere in the shop would provide answers.

"Where is Mr Tempus?"
It shrugged.

"I need to find him," she said, placing it down again. She was shaking. "You'd better stay here."
The clock shook defiantly, and leapt enthusiastically into her open satchel. The other clocks in the racks came to life, clattering in a chorus of head-splitting alarms.

"What's going on up there?!" Sheridan called.

"Nothing," Letisha called, and turned back to the clocks. "I can't carry you all! If you can't tell me what happened to him I'll have to find out for myself."

The ringing changed to a panicked tone; they all seemed to scream one word: Danger.

She hurriedly closed the flap of her satchel and backed out of the door. She locked it, and buttoned the key safely into her pocket.

Letisha quickly collected the Waking Dream from the kitchenette where Mr Tempus had decided to stash it. An Otherworldly weapon might be of use, and the potion was all she had. She had been keeping her new book in the satchel anyway, so naturally it went with her.

With the clocks still rattling behind the door, she made her way back down the stairs to where Sheridan was waiting.

"What was that dreadful din?" He exclaimed.

"Nothing," she said quickly, trying to keep the panic out of her voice.

Sheridan stuck his nose in the air. "I smell... a new timepiece!"

At this, the little clock jumped out of Letisha's satchel into Sheridan's hands.

"Oh!" he cooed. "What an absolute darling! Where did you get it from?"

"Upstairs. We need to go."

"Can the clock come?" Sheridan asked hopefully, batting his buttery eyes.

Letisha sighed, as they both looked at her expectantly. She opened her bag and indicated the clock should get back inside. They then stepped onto the little porch and closed the door.

"It is quite a way to my house, Miss Tate," he sounded embarrassed as a realisation dawned on him. "I usually fly...I don't know how you'd feel about riding on this humble old dragon's back. It's a wee bit knobbly."

Letisha shivered and pulled her coat thankfully around her. She secured her hat on her head, before looking at him and giving a little smile. "Walk, or a bumpy ride on a dragon's back. Those are my choices?"

12

A BUMPY RIDE

Letisha had a few moments to explore, as Sheridan appeared to be tying himself in knots as he adjusted his scarf.

The sky was perfect inky blue with stars of all different colours. She could vaguely make out fields, hills, and the twinkling of lights in the distance. To her left and right, other struggling candles lit other porches much like her own. Below, an infinite abyss stretched into nothing. Had she dropped a penny, she doubted it would ever reach the bottom.

She began to look up to survey the situation above her. She felt her stomach quiver as her foot slipped. Before she knew it, she was falling. For a few seconds she was too shocked to scream.

Sheridan turned dozily. "I'll just be a moment Miss Tate. Miss Tate?"

He looked around baffled, before it occurred to him what had happened. Without another thought, he thundered off the edge of the porch, and lurched into a nosedive.

Letisha's breath was torn away by the bitter air as her little body succumbed to gravity. The sky above slipped further away. She continued to scream but wasn't sure if anyone could even hear her, until she suddenly stopped falling. She felt a strong hand around her flailing ankle, before Sheridan began to hoist her back up towards the light.

They took a moment to catch their breath.

"Don't you ever scare me like that again, Letisha Tate!" Sheridan quivered. "I haven't the constitution to deal with such a fright!"

Letisha patted his hand even as she sobbed. "That was very brave of you, Sheridan. You saved my life."

"I did?"

"Of course. It was my stupid fault to get so close to the edge," she admitted, trying to quell her own shuddering

"There, there," Sheridan said. "I've been asking Mr Tempus for years to get a fence. This will be an eye opener for him!"

"If we ever find him," Letisha sniffed sadly.

"Best we get going," he said, going onto all fours so Letisha could climb on. "Is your bag all buckled and secure?

"Yes." Letisha climbed on and wiggled into a groove between two of the larger horns on his back. He spread his wings out either side of her, testing her position for comfort. "Alright; let's go."

Sheridan drove forward on all fours at formidable speed, and took off with a beat of his great pink wings. He was air-bound before she could blink. Within seconds they had climbed more than fifty feet. Behind her Letisha could see the back porch of Mr Tempus's shop as it was in her world. From this side it appeared quite flat, just a brick wall with a door, and next to it on either side were rows and rows of doors and porches varying in colour and size. The sky behind was blue fading into black, an unnaturally smooth colour. Letisha felt quite disorientated.

"Are all those…." She trailed off.

"Portals? Oh yes," Sheridan called back.

"Why are there so many?"

"Well, it wasn't always so; when I was young there were only about a hundred, but then one day, I noticed a few more, and over the years since I have been coming they have just multiplied. Strange really."

"Where do they go?"

"There are Portals all over your world, and all over ours. There are tales of multiple worlds and all number of creatures moving about and living their lives behind those doors. This just happens to be where a lot of them come in. As I recall, the one two doors down from yours comes out somewhere in China!"

"Do they all go into watchmaker's?"

"Oh no, it was a nice tea shop, actually. They invited me in and we had a lovely chat, when I strayed through once by accident."

"You speak Chinese?"

"No. They spoke dragon."

"Oh."

"Different dialect, mind you. Hold on, you might want to put your hood up, we're about to get wet!"

They were heading right into a dense black cloud. Letisha nudged her satchel.

"Are you alright in there, clock?"

She was met with a faint but satisfied chiming. Letisha pulled her hood up over her hat, as a few huge raindrops fell on her hands as she clutched Sheridan's scarf. She tried to rub the fears of flying on a dragon's back from her mind. Nobody would ever believe her about this journey; it was a secret she added to a growing collection. It was the kind of wild experience some children never even dreamed about, and yet here she was, the wind rushing past her ears and tugging at her hair and clothes while Sheridan chatted politely. She could hear in his voice how excited he was to have a passenger who had so much to learn about the Otherworld,

"Don't you get scared in stormy weather?" Letisha quaked as a huge thunderclap rattled about them.

"Not really," he called back. "Dragons don't conduct electricity." Letisha wondered how many interesting facts he actually knew about dragons, but since she hadn't been able to pinpoint his age, she imagined his knowledge could be infinite. Her eyes streamed as Sheridan gained momentum in the thinning rain.

"How fast are we going?"

"Pardon?"

Letisha tried not to choke as the air sped past her. "How fast can you fly?"

"We're only going about sixty miles an hour," Sheridan said, but beat his wings harder and began to speed up. "I can go up to a hundred and eighty if you like!"

"No, no, sixty is fine," she peeped nervously.

"Would you like to see me do a loop-di-loop?"

"Wouldn't I fall off?"

"Oh, yes," Sheridan agreed. "Sometimes I forget about gravity." They continued in silence as the clouds began to clear. Above them, Letisha could see a sky full of stars and below them the occasional glow of a house or two. There were few roads to speak of, and no streetlights. The view was quite different to that at home.

"Are there many other dragons here?"

"That depends on how you define 'many'. Our families are vast but we like our space," Sheridan called back. "Uncle Sigmund and I are a rarity, living together just the two of us. He is old and he won't admit he needs help sometimes. Dragons are sociable creatures and they love their parties. Normally they like to travel in Puffs."

"Puffs?"

"You never heard the term 'a Puff of Dragons'? Like a 'pack of wolves' or a 'murder of crows'?"

"No."

"'Puff' is the collective term for dragons. What is the collective term for little girls?"

"I don't think there is one." Letisha admitted.

"Well, we must think of one!" Sheridan exclaimed, clasping his hands enthusiastically and temporarily letting go of Letisha's legs. She screamed and toppled sideways, even as he caught her in the nick of time.

"So sorry!" he cried. "It's been so long since I had a friend visit. I hope you'll like Uncle Sigmund."

"What's he like?"

"Almost as old as the earth itself," Sheridan said grandly. "You must be on your very best behaviour and mind your manners. He's very particular about that."

"Is he as bad as Mrs Grisham's Ghost?"

"Not at all. I didn't realise you'd met the old dear."

"Unfortunately. She called me a scoundrel."

Sheridan groaned. "As I recall I am 'a brute and a great brainless lug'. Amongst other things."

"Will I see any other dragons?" Letisha asked. She had had enough of Mrs Grisham's Ghost.

"'Not likely in this weather," returned Sheridan shortly.

Letisha pointed to a formation below, which she could only describe from such a height as horned birds. "What about those?"

"Well, perhaps." Sheridan said, rolling his yellow eyes.

"Do they speak Dragon or English?"

Below, the Puff of Dragons flew in an arrow shaped formation like geese. The moon shone off their backs and she could see their colours; some were moss green like Sheridan, some were pale blue like a calm ocean, and some were rusty red. They were silent and incredibly graceful; from where Letisha saw them it was difficult to believe that each one could easily weigh more than a ton. As they passed over a river, their lustrous bellies reflected in the water.

Letisha had to remind herself that she wasn't dreaming. A ripple of excitement mixed with fear tingled along each nerve.

"Couldn't we just say hello?" she tried not to beg.

"I don't know about that," Sheridan said, lowering his voice. "Firstly we have work to do, and secondly I'm not even sure about how they will react to you. I am used to interacting with humans, but some dragons are not so privileged. They might think that you are stupid and insolent, so it is best not to bother them, for now."

"Oh." Letisha said, disappointed. "I thought dragons were well-mannered."

"Yes, that's true."

"So why can't we speak to them? Will they really think I'm stupid?" She sighed. "All my teachers think I'm stupid."

Sheridan lowered his voice. "You remember when I said that there are certain rules about me bringing you here?"

"Are we breaking rules?"

"Surprisingly, I have never brought a mortal to the Otherworld before. All I suggest is that we keep a low profile until we get home. Uncle Sigmund will be most obliging to help Mr Tempus." He broke off, released one of her legs and pointed ahead. "Look there, yonder!"

Letisha squinted in the darkness, and could make out a tiny glowing shape ahead, like a jack-o'-lantern perched atop a tall, crooked hill. They dropped lower as Sheridan prepared to land

"What is it?" Letisha asked.

"That," Sheridan said proudly. "Is Bin Rist."

*

Aunt Stackhouse thundered down Covert Street like a hell-bound locomotive. She was on her way to stir up more trouble for her niece, unable to bear the little misfit having such an enjoyable summer.

She listed the things on which she would quiz Letisha, to see if she had actually learned anything.

"Peter Tempus!" she shrieked as she found the front door locked, with so much rage and nowhere to vent it. "I demand you open this door; it is well past opening time!"

The shop was silent and still. Aunt Stackhouse growled; she did not like being ignored. She glared to the left, then to the right, and decided that the entry was her best bet. She stomped towards it, her plain shoes echoing off the damp bricks.

When she arrived at the slightly open back door, she grinned deviously to herself. Declining anything so polite as knocking, she simply pushed the great door open and stepped inside.

The empty room was bitterly cold. Her ragged breath almost froze in the air as she surveyed the room in the darkness. For one fateful second, Aunt Stackhouse sensed she was not alone in the room. She barely had a moment to scream before a rough sack was pulled over her head. Everything went black.

13

BIN RIST

"Bin Rist," Sheridan said as they landed, "has been my family home for thousands of years. It's the most beautiful place in all the worlds."
Letisha couldn't really see much in the darkness. Sheridan's house was perched atop the most peculiar hill, which felt fragile and metallic underfoot as he let her down.

"I'll let you stretch your legs." Sheridan advised. They had been travelling for almost an hour. Letisha climbed down, yawning. The little clock jingled in her satchel, so she took it out and let it run around her feet. Sheridan was already making his way up the steps. Letisha followed him with some difficulty. She scooped up the clock for the climb.

"Where did that remarkable clock come from, anyway? And why is it so interested in you?"

"I don't know, but I've never had a pet before," she shrugged.
Though she had been sworn to secrecy, Letisha ached to tell Sheridan about Mr Tempus's secret occupation as Father Time, since she had an idea this was the reason he had vanished so suddenly. From what little she knew from playing cops and robbers, thieves stole things, not people.
Suddenly Sheridan's shining teeth and sharp claws seemed like little more than decoration; he was a gentle creature with a big heart, even if he was crazy when it came to watches. Still, she vowed to keep the secret, lest she get into more trouble.
Sheridan held her hand as the stairs became steeper, pulling her up some of the larger steps, like her father did when she was little. Sheridan made her feel so tiny, where everyone at home went on about how fast she was growing.

The hillside was formed of loose rocky crags, some sharp, some round. Letisha tried to imagine what it would look like in the light; perhaps it was a yellow colour, as some of the damp rocks glistened like gold in the moonlight. It must be almost lunchtime, she thought, yet there was still no sign of the sunrise.

Without the distraction of flying, Letisha's mind returned to Mr Tempus. What could an old dragon in another world possibly know do? Right now, she wasn't taking anything for granted.

After much huffing and puffing Letisha stood on yet another wooden porch, this time stained with a golden oak colour. A gas lamp mounted on the wall burned, glazing the porch in welcoming golden light. The curtains were drawn but there were lights on inside, and somebody was singing.

Sheridan slotted a silver key into a keyhole higher in the door than Letisha could reach. This door was much larger than the portaland easily half as wide again. Sheridan fitted through easily, with Letisha staying close to his side.

Sheridan removed his scarf and pulled on a pair of enormous tartan slippers. Letisha took off her boots and coat. Sheridan hung it on the gargantuan coat stand for her, next to his own belongings.

"I'd best go through first and let Uncle know you're here," Sheridan said. He disappeared through a door immediately to their left, and she briefly savoured the light and a delicious smell that filtered through. He closed the door behind him, and left Letisha standing in the hall where she squinted in the dim light at the monster of a house; it was easily five times the size of a large human house, with tall stairs leading off to numerous other floors, and paintings in gilt frames adorning the walls. Letisha admired the portrait of a tall elegant dragon with a long neck, and a conical hat perched between her – Letisha assumed it was a 'her' – long green ears. A gold necklace with a huge blue diamond adorned her throat, and her clawed fingers glittered with garnets and pearls. There was something terrifyingly beautiful about the whole display.

Sheridan cleared his throat from the doorway.

"Uncle is not happy; he said if he had known you were coming he would have baked a cake."

He held open the door for Letisha to enter. She felt her heart in her throat, praying that dragons were as courteous as Sheridan kept telling her. For all she knew, there was already a meat dish full of vegetables and dripping just big enough for her waiting next to the oven.

Letisha guiltily dismissed the idea. Sheridan was just as worried about Mr Tempus as she was, and when he was found he wouldn't be best pleased if Letisha had been trussed up and devoured like a Christmas ham.

When she had recovered from the blast of heat from a gargantuan fireplace, Letisha stopped dead as she beheld another dragon, grey-green and wearing a snow-white apron. He was even bigger than Sheridan, eyeballing her like a hungry wolf eyeballs a sheep as she entered the room.

"Ah, Miss Tate at last," Uncle Sigmund greeted her. A long wiry beard dangling from his craggy chin wobbled when he talked. He extended a clawed hand. She curtseyed slightly as she shook it, not knowing how else to react. "My nephew has told me so much about you. If I'd have known you were coming I would have baked my best Queen Cake, but I'm afraid we'll have to settle with teacakes instead. Is that alright for you?"

"Yes…thank you," Letisha managed.

Uncle Sigmund produced a tray with three enormous teacakes almost as big as Letisha's face. "Would you like yours toasted?"

"Yes please," she bobbed a curtsey once again, hoping she didn't look as ridiculous as she felt.

Uncle Sigmund blew a blue flame across the buns, toasting them golden brown in an instant. He popped one onto a place and handed it to Letisha. Sheridan had already toasted his own and was smearing it greedily with jam. Uncle Sigmund raised an eyebrow at his nephew, implying that their guest had nowhere to sit. Embarrassed by his appetite, Sheridan cleared his throat and went into the kitchen. He returned with a giant saucepan, which he placed upside down next to a second empty chair. The living room was arranged so they could sit around and talk while enjoying the warmth of the fire. A large patterned rug decorated the tiled floor and the walls were hung with more paintings, and a few tapestries. Everything was truly gargantuan in size; even if Letisha stood on her toes she would not reach the opposite side of the coffee table with her fingertips. The house felt as though it belonged to a very old couple who treasured everything they owned and were firm believers in 'make do and mend'. Letisha noticed that the chairs had been patched and darned, and none of the plates or cups matched. It was the most charming room she had ever seen.

"You could take my chair if you want, but I thought it might be a bit high," he handed her the cushion from behind him. "This will make you more comfortable."

Letisha thanked him and placed the much-repaired cushion down as she stood to help herself to jam from the coffee table. The little clock was preparing to curl up in front of the fire. It was all very civilised; Letisha admired an enormous gramophone taking pride of place in one corner of the room, which Uncle Sigmund wound up for her to listen to while they ate; he explained that it was a recording of one of his own performances on the harpsichord.

After they had finished eating, Uncle Sigmund ushered Sheridan and Letisha from the room, along with the little clock, disturbed from its sleep. He claimed to have a fabulous meal to prepare, to which Sheridan added,

"If there's one thing dragons love more than good manners, it's a fabulous meal."

Sheridan showed Letisha around, explaining that the house had once upon a time been home to more dragons of the great Adelinda Clan. They had all long since moved on to greener pastures, his parents included. He and his uncles' existence was one of intellectual pursuits and collecting.

They passed room after room dedicated to various activities. One housed Uncle Sigmund's harpsichord, and other outsized instruments. Another was full of more books than Letisha had ever seen some of which Sheridan told her were older than his uncle. There was a room that looked like a laboratory, but was used for making jams, marmalades and preserves. Sheridan referred her to a book his uncle had written years ago concerning the topic, but not the secret recipes themselves.

Letisha noticed that every room had proper light fittings, such as she might see at home, only none were working; each bulb had a candle melting onto it.

"I didn't expect dragons to have electricity," she remarked at such an odd sight.

"Why ever not? You have it, don't you?"

"Well yes, but I didn't think…"

"You should always think, and always ask questions; that's how we learn. We used to have electricity, a long time ago, but since this dreadful weather has set in nothing works. Luckily we can wind up the gramophone, and the range only needs fuel. It's been so long we just started buying candles again."

At the end of the tour they came to Sheridan's most beloved room. He held the golden doorknob expectantly, indicating that Letisha read the plaque.

"The Collecting Rooms," she said. The little clock jumped excitedly in her hands.

"You're the first person to see this, you know," Sheridan said mysteriously as he opened the door. They stood in another room, with a green door either side of them. One was labelled 'Sheridan' and the other 'Sigmund'.

"We each have a room to house our collections. Mine is all timepieces, but Uncle likes all sorts of things."

"What sort of things?" Letisha couldn't resist asking.

"Oh, I don't know; books, coins, stamps, bottles, recipes…you name it, he's either got a collection or is about to begin one." Sheridan explained. "Of course his timepiece collection is much bigger than mine, but it's also a lot messier."

Sheridan opened the door just a crack. The contents moved and groaned, as if a great pile of junk were pressing against it, willing to be released. Letisha could see all the various objects of Uncle Sigmund's collection, shining bottles, a handful of watches, scrolls of paper and books. All were simply dumped together in a veritable galaxy of collector's chaos.

"See?" Sheridan grunted and heaved with all his might to close the door.

Letisha gasped, then chuckled.

Sheridan turned to his own door, which opened comfortably. He breathed fire left and right to ignite candles atop the ornate fittings lining the walls. The candles were set between dozens of glass cabinets that housed hundreds upon hundreds of watches. She walked forward into the room, her shoes echoing on the polished floor. Sheridan closed the door and followed her in.

"What do you think?"

"It's amazing," she breathed quietly. "How long have you been collecting?"

"Oh, years now; I used to admire my father's collection, and when he left he passed it on to me. I've been adding to it ever since!"

Letisha stopped at a cabinet housing a very ancient stone sundial.

"It took your world a long time to catch up on how to build watches our way, but even the first timekeepers got the methods right," Sheridan explained. "I am fascinated by the science of time; it is precious. It can be saved, wasted, spent, given and taken. Mr Tempus has saved me so much time over the years; it would have taken a lot longer to build my collection were he not so good at acquiring fine timepieces." Sheridan took the watch that had formerly been Letisha's from his wrist and chose a space for it in the cabinet behind them. "I am proud to add this piece to my collection. I am considering starting a Plastics section."

"So you have electricity," Letisha mused. "But no plastic."

"Well, sometimes we overtake you, sometimes you overtake us," Sheridan shrugged. "It's funny like that."

The little clock wagged its behind enthusiastically, jumping from Letisha's hands and making a dash. The room was so long it was panting, as much as it was able, by the time it got to the back.

"Goodness," Letisha gasped as she regarded a tall cabinet, hidden in a corner with no candles and covered with a thick layer of dust. "I thought you prized your collection."

"I do," Sheridan retorted. "But it's hard taking care of something so big. Here," he pulled a candle from the wall and held it up to the cabinet. Letisha brushed off some of the dust, enabling them to view the treasures inside.

"Ah!" Sheridan exclaimed, throwing a streak of hot wax onto the floor. "These are some of my oldest watches. Well, the oldest watches, dating back to the 16th Mortal Century!"

He turned a tiny ornate key and opened the cabinet, so that the primitive timepieces could be viewed more clearly.

"These are from a time when mortal men were just grasping the art of keeping time in style. Behold," he exclaimed, pointing to what Letisha saw as a wooden box filled with intricate cogs. "The Marine Chronometer, able to determine longitude by means of celestial navigation! It's simply delicious!"

Letisha's attention was drawn to a particularly ordinary looking pocket watch, lost at the bottom corner of the cabinet. It had a simple gold case, and an engraved decorative swirl, and three crystals set into the surface. It was oddly familiar.

"May I touch them?" Letisha asked.

"Of course. If Mr Tempus trusts you, then so do I!"

Letisha nodded, and reached in to take the pocket watch. It fitted into her hand comfortably and was slightly warm to the touch, despite the cold of the room around them. She ran her hand over the smooth surface, feeling the little bumps of the coloured crystals. She admired the blue crystal, which was larger than the others. It was also more vibrant.

Still holding the watch in her hand, she sat down and took the book from her bag. She flicked to the page she had so recently been looking at with Sheridan.

"Oh glory, my best Swiss Lever Escapement!" he cooed at his collection.

"Um, Sheridan." Letisha began.

"Invented by a gentleman named Mr Mudge…"

"Sheridan."

"In Seventeen Fifty Nine as I recall, I remember it well!"

"Sheridan, look!" Letisha cried, tugging him down. He gazed blankly for a moment until her words sank in. The watch she held was identical to the illustration in the book.

"Oh joy!" he cried. "What a fabulous discovery! I knew I had one! Didn't I say so?"

Letisha laid the book down on the floor, as Sheridan dropped down beside her with a thump. She scanned over the instructions that the author had presented with the drawings.

"Can you read these out to me, please?" She asked, handing him the book.

Sheridan obliged; "'To open the Ouroboros to the Second Face, compress the central movement and turn back the hour hand by half an hour. What an odd thing to do."

Letisha followed the instructions. The watch vibrated momentarily before the First Face snapped back on an invisible hinge, revealing a Second Face. Eight cogs had been forged in shimmering gold, as well as numerous other movements that ticked and chuntered. In the book, each one was labelled with a different function, though the cogs themselves were blank. It indicated that the bearer of the Ouroboros would need to memorise its functions to use it successfully. The illustration showed cogs for speed, give, take, storage, stop and start, past, future and erase.

A central vial was half-filled with a bubbling green viscous liquid. It danced and shimmered in the dim candlelight, almost as if it had a will of its own.

Sheridan's eyes lit up as they both gazed upon the glowing Second Face of the Ouroboros, fascinated and bedazzled.

Without another word, Letisha referred to the book once more and opened the Ouroboros to the final face, which once again was an intricate mass of cogs and gears. It was both chaotic and beautifully harmonious; every action affected another, or it would have were the cogs moving. The watch was quite dead, despite a low ticking that emitted somewhere from within its workings. In this face, the cogs were adorned with a gold scroll.

"All the labels are empty," Letisha pointed out. "According to the book, the owner's name will appear on the central cog, but this has nothing. Shouldn't your name be on here, Sheridan?"

"Well, I never really owned it," Sheridan admitted. "I remember Mr Tempus asked me to store it for him, where it would be out of sight. He was quite insistent that I kept it a secret, so you see why it's been tucked away in here."

"But where did he get it from?" Letisha asked quietly. The little clock also waddled up to have a look.

"I have no idea," Sheridan admitted. "I recall bringing it home, after he told me that it was very old and valuable. But I didn't pay for it…"

Letisha narrowed her eyes, remembering how she had found him in the stock room. "You didn't steal this, did you?"

"I most certainly did not! Mr Tempus said that he couldn't sell it to me, but that I was trustworthy enough to be its guardian. I shouldn't even be showing you," Sheridan paused, casually passing his index finger through the candle's flame. He asked at last. "So, what shall we use it for?"

"What?"

"Oooh, I could make myself younger!" he clapped his hands.

"Sheridan, that's not what it's for. According to this book it shouldn't even exist."

Suddenly Sheridan was very serious, remembering his solemn promise to Mr Tempus. He took the watch from Letisha and closed it carefully.

"Come," he took up the book and stood, pulling her to her feet with his free hand. "We should inform Uncle Sigmund."

14

A WISE OLD DRAGON'S TALE

Clean copper pots sat gleaming atop the glowing range after Sheridan had completed the washing up. Letisha had attempted to help but most of the plates were made of heavy pewter, so instead Sheridan set her to polishing the cutlery as he began boiling water for tea.

"So," said Uncle Sigmund. "It seems Mr Tempus is in trouble, and there is a great deal more to his dilemma than we were able to decipher, until now. What do you know about this, Miss Tate?"

"Well," Letisha began. "I woke up as normal and found the shop empty. Mr Tempus has never been late opening as long as I've been staying with him, so I went downstairs to see what was going on, and I found Sheridan…" she stopped herself, knowing that Sheridan might get in trouble if his uncle found out what he had been doing. "….and he was looking for Mr Tempus too. The shop was a mess, as if somebody had been searching for something."

"I helped to tidy up," Sheridan added.

"I see," said Uncle Sigmund, scratching his chin. "And do you know why Mr Tempus might have been taken in this way?"

Letisha shrugged. "I have no idea."

Uncle Sigmund bent down, his long horned neck coiling his head towards Letisha. She sensed he suspected that she was not telling the whole truth, but she tried to hide her discomfort.

"How much has Mr Tempus told you, my dear?"

Letisha felt the colour draining from her face; she could not hide her secrets. He did not wait for her to confess anything, squinting through his clouded milk bottle glasses. His beard twitched.

"In the beginning, when the world was young and we dragons were not yet hatched, and mortal men were barely thought of, the three Architects were each laden with a gift. A gift of great power, and a terrible burden.

"Using their wares and their gifts, the Architects built the world you see. Mother Earth filled the world with life, helped along by Jack Frost, who sent seasons to oversee the cycle of life Mother Earth had created. Father Time governed the very grains of time, enslaving us all to the hands of a great clock."

"So what you're saying," Letisha interrupted. "Is that Mother Earth and Jack Frost are ruled by Father Time."

"No, child, you misunderstand," said Uncle Sigmund. "They are all controlled not by Father Time, but by the duty of their Ouroboros. Whosoever holds the Ouroboros may control time over all the others. It is told that an Ouroboros is susceptible to a person's emotions and his past; when the owner has good thoughts and is happy, the Ouroboros remains pure. Equally if his thoughts are evil and selfish, the Ouroboros become corrupt. Despite this, it is only when the three Ouroboros are used in harmony the very fabric of life also works in harmony."

"So whose watch does Sheridan have, and why?"

"There is a legend we tell. Mother Earth and Father Time had once been harmonious as husband and wife, but they grew apart, and finally they broke apart. Father Time cast Mother Earth aside, accusing her of secretly living a mortal life."

Letisha asked. "Why would she want to do that if she was so powerful?"

"Because women are mysterious creatures," Sheridan suggested.

"Because," Uncle Sigmund continued, not in the least impressed at being interrupted, "I believe that Father Time is very cruel, and makes fools of us all. Mother Earth can also be cruel, but she is also creative, and thrives amongst beauty and progress. Time is unchangeable, where nature is not. I believe she left Father Time and possibly even gave up her power as an immortal to be with a mortal man whom she loved. It is believed that they had a son."

Maybe Uncle Sigmund knew more than she realised. He seemed to know an awful lot about the Architects. Letisha was puzzled.

"How do you know all this is true, if it happened at the beginning of time?"

"No, no, child," he said. "They received their Ouroboros at the beginning of time. Mother Earth only gave up her immortal power a short time ago. It's probably only been a hundred years or so, well within my lifetime."

He cleared his throat, pausing to remember his place in the story. "Now, it is also believed that Jack Frost loved Mother Earth. They built the seasons together, and he doted on her and set about winning her affections. He gave everything he could in our world and yours, his every possession, including...."

"My Ouroboros!" cried Sheridan. "Oh, why did Mr Tempus not tell me how special it was?"

"I imagine he wanted it kept safe," said Uncle Sigmund. "So do stop swinging it around like that, Sheridan."

"Sorry," Sheridan clutched the Ouroboros securely.

"That's why you're stuck in permanent winter," Letisha exclaimed. "So where is Jack Frost now?"

"Nobody knows," said Sheridan, and then giggled. "But he's not getting his watch back! It's mine now!"

"It is certainly not yours," said Uncle Sigmund sternly. "You are its guardian. This Ouroboros is the rightful property of Mr Tempus."

"But surely," Letisha went on. "Returning the Ouroboros to Jack Frost would restore everything to normal, if it is just a matter of using the watches in harmony. And what about Mother Earth's Ouroboros? Did she give that up when she chose a mortal life? Is Father Time in control of everything now? Where is Mother Earth's Ouroboros?" She took a breath at last. "And if she did love a mortal man over a hundred years ago he would be dead now wouldn't he?"

"How tragic!" Sheridan interjected, placing a hand to his brow melodramatically.

"Too many questions." Uncle Sigmund removed his glasses and polished them with a handkerchief as big as a tea towel. "Life is never so simple as all that." He did not venture to say anything further, until Letisha opened her mouth to speak, where he interrupted her.
"You are young, Letisha. There is much about your own world that you do not understand, let alone ours. Best to let sleeping dragons lie."

There was an awkward silence. Sheridan cleared his throat, taking the brass kettle off the heat as it began to whistle. The gramophone slowed to an uncomfortable pace, the music slurring along with great difficulty. Letisha assumed that Uncle Sigmund did not like to be
argued with, and she also knew that she was about to argue. In her little human eyes a reflection of the firelight danced, along with the rebellious spark of youth. Sheridan braced himself for fireworks.

"Mr Tempus is my friend," she said in a low and very calm voice. "And he is missing."

"He is mortal. These things happen." Uncle Sigmund replied stiffly.

"What if he has been kidnapped, though? I'm sure it's to do with that watch. Whoever took him might have been looking for it, if it's so special. Mr Tempus is only the guardian of a Portal, and there are hundreds of them. If somebody didn't take him, and wasn't looking for something valuable, then why had the stockroom been turned inside out?"

"Nobody but the Architects knows about the Ouroboros, my girl." Uncle Sigmund grunted.

"Except you."

"Well, yes…"

"And Mr Tempus."

"Well…"

"And whoever wrote that book."

"Oh,"

"And now me, and Sheridan too." She folded her arms when she knew she had him beat. "At least that narrows down the list of suspects. Wouldn't you agree?"

Uncle Sigmund shuffled awkwardly, mottled scales bristling. In his discomfort he looked like an older version of his nephew. He leaned in very close and sniffed Letisha slightly. She could feel the heat of his breath on her face.

"As long as your alleged 'kidnapper', whoever they are, doesn't get hold of the Ouroboros, things will remain as they are," Sigmund concluded rigidly.

"Depressing, desolate and permanently in the grip of this unnatural winter," said Sheridan glumly.

"And that's a good thing?!" Letisha demanded. The tension in the room spiked.

"I find the cold bracing," said Uncle Sigmund. "Don't you, Sheridan?"

"Actually…" Sheridan began, looking nervously from his uncle to Letisha. "I get so many colds and sore throats in this weather, and I have such a long throat, Uncle. I think something ought to be done."

At this point Letisha got up and stood next to Sheridan. Uncle Sigmund wrinkled his scaly brow into a frown, making him look all the more terrifying. Letisha jumped as a twig cracked on the fire.

Uncle Sigmund sighed, deflated. "Your best bet is Selena. If something has upset the balance that the Ouroboros put in place, you can bet she will know about it."

"Selena…the enchantress?" Letisha asked, confused.

"The enchantress." Uncle Sigmund did not question how Letisha knew who Selena was. "Sheridan, you will accompany Letisha to Tempera-Sleus; you will find the enchantress Selena there."

"But Uncle," protested Sheridan. "You know I am… scared of the enchantress,"

Letisha gasped. "But you're a dragon. How scary can an enchantress be?"

"Selena has powers beyond our understanding, child," said Uncle Sigmund. "Sheridan is right to be afraid. But she is also a friend to the creatures of this world, especially the dragons, and she understands it like nobody else. If something is amiss, if somebody is doing something they shouldn't, word will get back to her in one way or another. Equally, Mr Tempus is mortal like you, and it won't go unnoticed that he has passed into her world. Selena will point you in the right direction."

"But she won't have forgotten that I once tried to eat her orb," Sheridan moaned, wringing his hands. "Uncle, please don't make me go. I'll…I'll not buy any watches for a month!"

"Selena is real?" Letisha managed, hardly able to believe her ears. She had kept her promise for so long she had become convinced that she had dreamed Selena up.

"Of course Selena is real," said Uncle Sigmund. "What a ridiculous question."

Letisha decided it would do no good in explaining that not only had she met the 'terrifying' Selena before, but that it had happened in the comfort of her own world. She could see that Uncle Sigmund liked being all-knowing, so she kept her word to the enchantress instead. She took Sheridan's hand in hers.

"Please come with me? Think of how much Mr Tempus has done for you. Who's going to take care of me if we don't find him?"

Sheridan looked at her with butter coloured eyes. He squeezed Letisha's hand.

"Sheridan J. Adelinda at your service." He stood up proudly, fluttering his wings a little. "Now, how about we move onto the more important business of getting some tea and biscuits on the go?"

*

"So who else lives at Tempera-Sleus?" Letisha asked, examining a map that Uncle Sigmund had produced for her to look at while Sheridan fussed over refreshments. His stomach really was bottomless.

"Oh, only a handful of witches and enchantresses, and they won't give you any trouble. It is Selena's realm and she keeps them in check."

Letisha couldn't keep the nervous wobble out of her voice. "Now when you say witches, I can't help but wonder…"

"You needn't fear, Letisha." Uncle Sigmund was unruffled. "If you say you are there on my business, all will be well. The Enchantresses and dragons tend to live and let live"

"And are these Enchantresses Oddfolk too?"

"They are not; for the better part, they are immortal, so they set themselves separately from the Oddfolk. Just like the Beldams do, but we don't see many of them so just put it out of your mind."

"Beldams?"

"Bad Witches," Sheridan cut in, before changing the subject. "Now, Puce, there's a place with some history."

The image on the map was adorned with an array of dragons who might have been red when the map was new, but were now faded to pink. They wore armour on their heads, chests and backs. The drawings were marvellously detailed; each dragon was unique.

"You've heard the story a thousand times, Sheridan," Uncle Sigmund sighed, rolling the map up abruptly even as Letisha was still exploring it.

"Oh go on, uncle. Don't go being a stick in the mud when we have a guest. Did you know," Sheridan turned to Letisha, his eyes glowing with pride, "That my Uncle was part of the final battle to bring peace between the Adelinda Clan and the Red Dragons of Puce?"

"Sheridan, you do embellish things," Uncle Sigmund snapped playfully, polishing his glasses once more. "It wasn't a battle, it was a conference, in which the territories were divided up accordingly. We vowed to no longer squabble over such silliness. There are more important goals to be achieved than winning fights."

Letisha put a head on her hand and sighed, "I think you should come and talk to the boys at my school. One word from you and they'd never fight again."

Uncle Sigmund drew himself up and boomed in a mighty voice;

"Light is day, and dark is night,

"And nevermore shall dragons fight,

"For in the end when all's said and done;

"Preparing a feast is much more fun."

He slumped down and dipped a ginger biscuit in his tea.

Sheridan offered Letisha another biscuit, which she declined politely. He had told her about dragons and their appetites many times, though she was glad to learn that dragons did not eat people. Their palate was much more sophisticated, and they loved to cook. The biscuits he offered her were as big as saucers – quite dainty by dragon standards - and the ginger was hotter than any she had ever tasted. Such was their nature she supposed that dragons liked spicy food.

"Food and naps," Sigmund added. "Which reminds me, isn't it about time all good little mortals scuttled off to bed? You have a big day ahead of you and I don't want you yawning and offending the Oddfolk."

Letisha cast her eyes up at him and he answered her question before she could even ask.

"The Oddfolk are the creatures of the Otherworld; those who do not fall into the genus of Dragons or Immortals. Do I need to find my Compendium of Creatures? Or was that perfectly clear?"

"Perfectly," she yawned, suddenly realising just how tired she felt. Exhaustion weighed on her and she longed for a pillow like never before. Sheridan stood and offered Letisha a hand, which she took gratefully. She swayed a little as she stood, her eyes heavy.

"Let's see if we can find a place to put you," Sheridan said, opening the door and leading her towards the stairs.

*

Mr Tempus had never felt so cold.
He was so far relying on every sense except sight, since he had been blindfolded. The bitter air nipped his flesh, and the stone floor made his feet ache. He had given up pushing against the bars that held him. They too were so cold he could not touch them for long without burning his fingertips.
With his hands bound and his body exhausted, his mind raced over methods of escape. Had there been a door with a lock, he might have picked it, but there were only icy bars.
When he was not fabricating escape plans, his mind raced back to the shop, where he prayed Letisha had not been taken too. Once or twice he had called out to her, thinking she might be in the cell with him.
He had no idea who his captor was, but he had a good idea. It was going to take a sensational plan to escape alone. It would take a miracle to get a message to Letisha.

GRAM-SHANK

Dawn broke in Bin Rist. Sheridan collected Letisha and helped her descend the stairs. They ate a quick breakfast of delicious porridge, which Letisha had never tried before since her parents couldn't make it without having it look like cement.

After breakfast, Sheridan tied on his best scarf as Letisha pulled on her boots, in between trying to scoop her clock into her satchel.

Uncle Sigmund surveyed the beautiful morning as he held the door open. The sky was cobalt blue and the sun shone, though there was still an arctic chill in the air.

"Remember," he said as Letisha climbed onto Sheridan's back. "We have little time to spare. You must go straight to Tempera Sleus. We can't have you gadding about with that Ouroboros in your bag."

The little clock jingled beside the book, a packed lunch, and the mysterious Ouroboros, which she had already been told to guard with her life. It had been safely zipped inside the deepest pocket of her bag, and was not to be taken out until they reached the forests of Tempera-Sleus.

"Of course, Uncle," Sheridan beat his wings. "We'll go straight there."

With that they soared into the air, leaving Uncle Sigmund waving in the doorway.

Looking back over her shoulder, Letisha was shocked to see that Sheridan's rickety house was not perched on top of a high hill, but on a mountain of gold and silver. An enormous mound of treasure glistened in the watery light. Atop the red-tiled roof, a battered weathervane turned slightly in the gentle wind, beside a crooked chimney that spat white smoke out into the sky. Only now did Letisha realise how truly bizarre the house was; it was made of brick, wood panels and even patches of metal here and there. If anything, it looked like several smaller houses had been cobbled haphazardly together to make something big enough for the dragons to live in. Just as Sheridan looked a little precarious when he flew, his house looked precarious perched on the hill.

"When you get to be as old as us," Sheridan explained, as she gawped at the hoard of treasure, "Money becomes of little importance. Ours is nothing compared to some of the hoards other dragons live on, but it will keep us going for a long while yet. You didn't think all that talk about dragons guarding treasure was a myth, did you?"

"Of course not," Letisha lied. "But doesn't anyone ever steal from it, just lying there?"

Sheridan grinned his toothy grin. "Would you steal from me?"

"No," Letisha admitted.

They were headed towards what looked like a huge green army. The forest emerged beneath them, as did the other marvels of the landscape.
There were lakes and pools, some as blue as forget-me-nots, others red and murky with mud. The trees appeared to change colour as the wind blew, ranging from rich green, to red, to gold, and back to green again.

Letisha frowned. "I thought you were stuck in permanent winter! Why are there still leaves on the trees?"

"Well, you wouldn't just expect them to stand naked in the cold, would you? Mother Earth gave our trees good sense; they know how to take care of themselves!"

"Is this what Uncle Sigmund meant when he said that the world was out of balance?"

"Precisely," said Sheridan, stumbling over the word slightly as the wind took his breath away.

"And is time affected too?" she asked, clinging to his back. "I can't seem to figure out how time works here; are there still twenty four hours in a day?"

"Sometimes,"

"Sometimes?!"

"Sometimes twenty four, sometimes twelve, sometimes six. Sometimes forty-eight. Those are the worst; I sleep for more than half the day!" he explained. "I think yesterday was only twelve hours."

"So what you're saying," Letisha went on, "Is that you collect watches and clocks even though they are useless in your world, as time itself has been thrown out of balance along with the seasons."

"I just think timepieces are so beautiful," admitted Sheridan. "Best of all, when I visit your world, all my watches work, as your time is normal. Have you checked your little clock? Perhaps it is capable of keeping the correct time."

"I think it's only keeping my time," Letisha said. She had no intention of getting it out of her bag so high up in case she dropped it. Sheridan was surprisingly steady, but she had no idea how turbulence affected dragons.

When they drew in to land about half an hour later, Letisha saw ahead of her a formation that reminded her of a mediaeval fair she had once visited on a school trip. Colourful tents with many sides and pointed tops were crowned with little flags that fluttered in the wind. This cluster was contained within what appeared to be the centre of a great walled town, with buildings large and small with thatched roofs and little smoking chimneys. Letisha struggled to take it all in; she had never seen anything quite like it in real life before, only in books whose pictures were not nearly so enticing as what she saw before her. In between these seemingly primitive structures were more modern buildings, resembling some of the older parts of her hometown. Letisha liked to think she knew what she was seeing, since her father was an expert on buildings, or so he said. He spent a great deal of time talking about things like neo-gothic and the romantic revival when they visited new places. She had never really listened, but was certain he would be fascinated by this place. It looked to have been cobbled together by a number of different builders with clashing ideas and no clue how to compromise, but somehow, it worked.

Some of the structures had tall turrets that would make the perfect home for a princess. Others had shining glass in their windows and doors, like ones she saw in church. The light danced on them as they passed. As Letisha saw her own reflection, she could not believe the sight of herself atop the back of a dragon.

Despite her belly being full of Uncle Sigmund's cooking, her mouth watered at the smell of roasting meat. This was mixed in with some kind of unusual floral perfume, and an unpleasant waste odour floating in the air.

"This is Gram-Shank," Sheridan called back. "It was built by the Faerie Lords of old, and has stood proud for hundreds of years."

Letisha tried to talk even as the wind bit at her tongue. "It's so pretty."

"That's only the foundation of the town. Gram-Shank is the centre of trade in this part of the Otherworld. The Oddfolk come from miles around to visit it. You're very lucky, you know!"

They touched down in the centre of the town, having flown over miles of cobbled streets and all manner of peculiar structures. Letisha was certain that even if she told people she had dreamed of such a place, they would not believe her.

As soon as they landed Letisha felt a great sense of confusion, since she almost stepped on a pair of tiny children. They were both impossibly thin and no taller than her calf, with large eyes and pointed hats. Their father just about came up to her knee. He pulled the children to his side, shook his fist at her and ranted in a language she did not understand, even as she tried to apologise.

"Watch your step! Look out for sprites!" Sheridan told her, carefully stepping around more tiny people. "You are by no means the smallest creature here."

"I'll do my best," Letisha pulled her bag out of the way as more sprites skipped past. They were cute, but quite devilish in appearance.

"Come along!" Sheridan began walking. "We have to get going!"

Letisha hung behind Sheridan as he trundled into the thick of the market. There were many languages being spoken, bartering, gossiping, arguing over prices and quality. It occurred to her that nobody here would understand English, and that this was about as foreign as foreign got to somebody who had barely travelled.

"So did you only speak Dragon before you met Mr Tempus? Did you learn from him?"

Sheridan roared with laughter. "My dear girl, the Oddfolk have been speaking a form of what you call English for centuries. Creatures have been passing between worlds long before you and I came along. You'll have no trouble here; everyone will understand you!"

Letisha nodded, even as she tried not to stare as a tiny man in a red jacket like a bellhop she had once seen at a hotel shot past on a fabulous pair of roller skates, waving an envelope importantly above his head. He wailed and dodged chaotically as a dragon riding an enormous penny-farthing bicycle went past, ringing a bell on the handlebars to clear the crowd. A tailcoat flapped behind him on either side of his tail, and he nodded his long head to Sheridan, who nodded back. He noticed Letisha lagging behind.

"There is no need to fear, Letisha. This is a day of celebration, so everyone is in a good mood."

"What are they celebrating?"

"The Festival of Bonfatum. It means 'good fate.'"

Letisha shrieked as a huge creature stepped over her, as she had had to step over the sprites. It had bushy eyebrows and a long moss-like beard. Fingers like twigs clutched a tankard of ale. The creature apologised in a deep baritone voice as it dodged out of her way.

"I'll take good care of you." Sheridan assured her.

Letisha was about to question his judgement, when a hefty fish was thrust under her nose, and a voice that shook her little body boomed,

"Best Gram-Shank Flounder, oak smoked and flavoursome as you like!"

Sheridan pushed the fish away as politely as possible as he surveyed the rest of the catch. "No thank you, my good sir. Have you any eels today?" Letisha frowned at the large hulking man made of mostly hair and earrings, pointing a finger as thick as a sausage tipped with a curved brown nail. She followed his finger as he offered his catch before becoming distracted by a tent at the end of the row that was adorned with colourful bunting that fluttered above the paths. It was hung so high she had to crane her neck to see properly. Tiny winged folk flitting and dancing in and out of the bunting. She tugged at Sheridan's waistcoat to ask him what they were, but he was too absorbed in his purchase to notice.

"I'll trade you for the mortal," grunted the fish-man.

"Not on your life," cried Sheridan, pulling Letisha close to his side. "She's not for sale."

"Two coins, then, in that case."

"That's extortionate!" cried Sheridan. "I know that eel is basically offal to you!"

"It's two coins, or the mortal," insisted the fish-man, licking his lips at Letisha. His teeth were like watermelon seeds. "Lovely with a bit of onion gravy."

"If I might interrupt," said Letisha quietly. She was trying her hardest to breathe through her mouth, since the fish did not smell particularly appetising and the fishmonger didn't smell much better. "Mortal isn't in season at the moment; I'm not at my most tender. Perhaps I could offer you something else for the eel?"

The fish-man folded his bulging arms, his curious face twisting. "I'm listening, mortal."

"What are you doing?" Sheridan hissed, clearly alarmed at her interjection. "Bartering with a troll?!" She took from her bag the lunch Uncle Sigmund had packed, including a little jar of lime and cardamom marmalade.

"This," she said, holding up the jar, "is the best thing to have at the moment. Keeps out the cold and easily worth two whole eels. It's all the way from Bin Rist, too." The fishmonger stroked his chins, and looked at her with one of his piggy black eyes narrowed. Without another word, he took two of his biggest eels and wrapped them in shiny brown paper. He handed them over to Sheridan, who in turn passed him the marmalade.

"Where did you learn to barter?" Sheridan marvelled as they left the troll behind.

"Mum does it at all the markets. She says you just have to convince people they're getting the better deal. He didn't smell like he'd ever had marmalade before, did he?"
Sheridan chuckled.

"Also," Letisha added, "He wouldn't really eat me, given the chance, would he?"
Sheridan bit his lip and was quiet. His silence made her uncomfortable, so she clung to his arm tightly. She tried not to stare at the creatures they passed; some of them were taller than Sheridan, with bulging arms and legs as thick as tree trunks, just like the one who had nearly squashed her. The smell of wood smoke hung about them. Some people were smaller than her, shimmering as they moved, and leaving a fragrance of cold, fresh air.

"What are those things?" Letisha found herself pointing at a creature who was somewhere between a man and a pile of boulders. He wore rough leather clothes and carried a roll of tools on his belt. His face was rocky and rough, little green eyes twinkling therein.

"That," Sheridan snapped, pushing her hand firmly down. "Is a Stoneworker; a giant."

"Oh."

"And you mustn't point. He's only going about his day at the fair, just like you." They carried on walking, and he went on. He nodded towards a creature who resembled a walking tree. "See that chap there? There are three types of giants; the Treekeepers, the Stoneworkers, and the trolls, who are the lesser of the three on all accounts."

"Sorry," Letisha said, embarrassed. She stepped aside as more people moved past her. She decided that she must think of them as people, even though they were strange or hairy or scaly.

They passed a stall headed with a banner exclaiming 'Fairy Snuff'. The stall was covered with wooden bowls of sweet smelling crystals, each labelled with a little card describing the product. Letisha thought how much the stuff looked like the kali she could buy at home. The stall itself was so small that she had to crouch down to get a proper look. The stallholder picked up a bowl and offered it to her.

"Smell this one, me dear! 'Tis sweeter than a summers' wind!"
Letisha did as she was asked, and indeed the woman was right. She had stark white hair, as if a sheep had curled up on top of her head, though she was still only as tall as Letisha's knee. Her skin was as rough as leather and her teeth were all but missing.

"No thank you, madam sprite," Sheridan nodded civilly, gently pulling Letisha away.

"I was only being polite," Letisha said as they walked. "Like you said I should be…"

"I know I did, but if you don't know what you're buying I suggest you decline politely and move on. There's stuff on this market that even I don't understand!"

Letisha had visited a few markets before with her parents, but none so strange and vivacious as Gram-Shank. She looked around at the curious buildings; some were huge enough to accommodate dragons or even giants, and some so tiny they made her feel like a giant herself.

The celebration was in full swing, with songs being sung and flower petals being scattered. Creatures of all shapes and sizes danced and mingled harmoniously. In all her normality, Letisha had never felt so peculiar and out of place, as a small boy with pointed ears and hair like a tabby cat held out his hands and invited her to join in. She graciously declined as Sheridan had suggested, feeling her cheeks burning scarlet with embarrassment.

The tabby boy was not her concern for long. All too quickly, Letisha felt strong hands grab her, and she was thrust into the thick of the jig. Her head whirled with the noise and colour of the fair as she spun, passed from one creature to another, some nearer to human and some definitely not so. At one point she was passed to what she assumed was a Stoneworker, whose hands were so large she feared she might be crushed. She tried desperately not to recoil in fear and horror. Some of the Oddfolk were quite beautiful, their movements so graceful they glided rather than walked. Others were outlandish and grotesque, with large ears and twisted bodies. She began to feel the prickle of panic in the base of her stomach, creeping up her back, and quivering in her little hands.

Suddenly, Letisha realised that she had been expertly separated from Sheridan, and was alone in the market. Though she called out his name, the roar of the jig drowned out her cries, and she was left to the mercy of the Oddfolk.

16

THE DUKE OF QUILL

Letisha squeezed back the tears of fright welling in her eyes, frustrated that she could not keep her head. She was not much of a dancer at the best of times, being far too clumsy and unable to remember routines.

The music was thankfully building to a finale as Letisha spun off violently into an alley between a butchers' shop and small residence.

She cried and shook fiercely with the shock of being thrust out of the celebrations as quickly as she had been pulled in. She tried not to be angry with the Oddfolk, who according to Sheridan were only celebrating and inviting her to join them. She did not understand their games; people didn't just begin dancing with one another where she came from.

She realised that despite the festivities, the Otherworld was a dangerous place, especially for a young girl with no knowledge of the local customs. She remembered how her Dad would say 'when in Rome, do as the Romans do,' but unfortunately Letisha had no more idea of what the Romans did than she did about what the Oddfolk did.

Frantically she searched her satchel, making sure nothing had fallen out during the dance. The little clock looked dizzy as she moved it aside, thankfully finding that the Ouroboros was still in position. She breathed a sigh of relief, though her lungs burned as she tried to calm herself down.

"All the strangers in the world coming through the back door at once couldn't have prepared me for this," she muttered to the dazed-looking clock.

Her legs ached from dancing. Keeping up with Sheridan as he thundered along at a tremendous speed was near enough impossible; it was really no surprise she had lost him. It was hopeless calling out as the dance of the Oddfolk had carried her despairingly far up the road.

Letisha sank helplessly to her knees, clutching the satchel with the clock still jingling inside. She cried into the sweet-smelling leather, its texture reminding her of home. The clock purred beneath, comforting her in its own little way. Furiously, she wished she had asked to ride on Sheridan's back where nobody could grab her.

She felt so guilty for getting lost, picturing Sheridan wringing his hands and hysterically calling her over the din, drowned out by the music and laughter of the Oddfolk. 'Not only have I lost Letisha,' she imagined him fretting through floods of tears, 'But I have lost the precious Ouroboros too! What will Uncle Sigmund say?'

Letisha frowned; she had not come all this way to be burned to a crisp by an enraged dragon. There was work to be done if she was to go home safely with Mr Tempus in tow.

She shakily got to her feet, pins and needles pricking her legs. At the mouth of the alley the festivities were still raging. She didn't much fancy the idea of walking into another chaotic conga line. Behind her, she heard a door open. She turned to see a huge brutish-looking creature –another troll perhaps – depositing a bucket of bones and offal into a barrel. It overflowed with items Letisha didn't care to name. An animal skull tumbled out of the bucket and shattered on the ground.

Repulsed and horrified, Letisha screamed and fled from her hiding place despite what she might have to confront on the high street.   The Troll butcher was watching her as she looked back, more with confusion than hunger.

Before she had time to think, Letisha realised it was too late to stop; she was about to run into somebody. She bounced against the ground, the clock making a brassy 'ping' as it hit the cobbles shortly after her.

"Beg pardon, miss" said a soft voice. "Let me help you up."
Through the blur of yet more frustrated tears, Letisha took the hand that was offered to her. She forced back a scream as she saw the face of the man who had helped her up. He had a thick purple scar across half of his face. It passed straight over his left eye, which was completely white. His nose was crooked and bent, having been broken some years earlier. His remaining eye sparkled like a sapphire, and he cracked a grin to reveal perfect pearly teeth.

"Nelson, Duke of Quill," said the man, holding out a hand to Letisha.
It was missing its little finger. He noticed her expression, "Don't mind the battle wounds; they don't hurt like they used to!"
Gingerly Letisha shook his hand, but found she could not muster a reply.
The Duke smiled kindly.

"Don't worry, I'm not going to drag you into the dancing. Are you alright?"

Letisha swallowed, "I've lost my friend."

"Well I daresay we'll have no trouble finding him," the Duke smiled. "What's your name, Miss?"

"Letisha," she managed.

"Letisha" repeated the Duke, straightening up. He had knelt down to talk to her, as he was quite a lot taller than she, despite being quite bedraggled. "Come on, let's get searching."

Letisha hesitated; was going back out into the crowd with a complete stranger really such a good idea? She saw a thin rapier hanging from his belt, and wondered if it was used to start fights or finish them. He wore a dishevelled uniform and even had a couple of medals hanging at his breast. Despite numerous repairs to his ensemble, he held himself well and talked nicely. Most importantly, he didn't look like he wanted to eat her, which was a start. She decided he looked the most human and therefore could be trusted.

They walked back down the high street, to where Letisha had last seen Sheridan. The Duke kept his hand on Letisha's shoulder at all times, artfully steering her out of the way of the dancing Oddfolk. She clutched her satchel tight to her body, afraid somebody might try to take it from her.

The crowd thinned as they approached the town square. Letisha could barely contain her joy as she saw Sheridan. He was standing beside the fountain, wringing his tail in one hand and chewing the claws on the other. He was frantically scanning the crowd, his eyes glazed over with tears. She still thought it adorable that a dragon would even cry at all.

"There he is!" she pointed, and began to speed up. Sheridan noticed her as she spoke. He beamed.

But the Duke was not so happy to see Sheridan.

"Avast, vile beast!" he cried, drawing his sword and stepping in front of Letisha. Immediately she regretted not telling the Duke that her friend was a dragon. "Keeping this child to put in a stew, were you?

Sheridan stepped out, spreading his wings and arms in a fearsome gesture.

"Aye, foolish knight, and I shall add you to the pot as well!" He boomed, before blowing an impressive fireball into the air. The singing and dancing ceased, and a crowd was forming around where the dragon and the Duke approached each other.

The Oddfolk had begun an awful chant, and Letisha shrieked and tried to pull the Duke back by his coat tails. He turned and simply winked at her.

Glancing around at the crowds, Letisha suddenly realised that something was going on here; the Odfolk were expecting a fight, and the Duke and Sheridan were going to provide it. She couldn't stand the idea of Sheridan being run through by the Duke's silver sword, which whistled through the air as he waved it about his head, before finally running at Sheridan.

Sheridan was surprisingly quick; he ducked and flung the Duke over his shoulder. The Duke landed on a patch of grass, rolled and tried to stand. Sheridan placed one foot firmly on his chest.

"O, brave knight! You have fought well today, but you must now admit defeat, and promise that hereafter dragons and Oddfolk shall live in peace and harmony together!"

"I don't know," the Duke said, and Letisha could have sworn she saw Sheridan pressing his foot harder into the Duke's ribs. "Alright, alright," he relented at last. "You have my word, O noble dragon!"

With that, Sheridan stepped aside and helped the Duke to his feet. From where she was standing, Letisha saw them mutter to one another. Her heart pounded with excitement.

Sheridan and the Duke held their hands up together. The crowd had fallen silent.

"Creatures of Gram-Shank!" proclaimed the Duke. "Let it be known that there is no ill will between Dragons and Oddfolk. We shall be brothers henceforth!"

The crowd erupted into cheers and applause, as Letisha noticed that this was not a fight but a re-enactment of some ancient event. In the thick of the crowd, the dragons that were present were patted on the back and even hugged by some of the younger Oddfolk. Letisha wished she'd been let in on the secret.

Finally, Sheridan and the Duke joined her.

"Thank goodness you're alright!" Sheridan cried, squeezing her. Letisha looked at her toes and didn't know what to say.

"I believe she was dragged away by the dancers," said the Duke. "You know how they want everyone to join in, whether they want to or not."

"Indeed," Sheridan said. "I see you two have introduced yourselves. I hope you didn't frighten her too much, Nelson,"

"Of course not!" the Duke cried, clearly offended. "Anyway, how could she be frightened of me when she has you for a companion? She is a brave girl!"

"Wait," Letisha shook her head. "You know each other?"

"Of course!" Sheridan said. "We go back a long way. I knew he'd retired in Gram-Shank so when I couldn't find you I went straight into the Maidens Arms Inn and asked after him. He was of course just sipping his first pint of the day and immediately jumped to attention when I said I'd lost you!"

Sheridan turned to the Duke and warmly shook his hand. "How can I ever thank you, Nelson?"

"Think nothing of it, old friend," said the Duke. "Just knowing Letisha is in safe hands is thanks enough. It's not often I get to have an adventure these days!"

"But...but the fight... the 'avast foul dragon!'..." Letisha tried to get her facts right. "What was that about?"

"Ah," said Sheridan. "I suppose I never did explain what the festivities are all about. Today is the anniversary of the declaration of peace between dragons and Oddfolk, and how it changed all our fates for the better. Locals re-enact the final battle, where a golden-hearted dragon let a brave knight live, and they bowed to one another and brought about peace. Today's performers were nowhere to be found, so we thought a little emergency theatre was in order. I must say I enjoyed it."

"You scared me half to death!" Letisha cried. "I thought you were going to kill each other!"

"Well, I did wink at you," the Duke shrugged.
Letisha pouted and folded her arms, and she hoped that the Duke and Sheridan realised that she was not impressed by their theatrical outburst.

"Won't you join me for a bite to eat?" asked the Duke, attempting to cheer Letisha up.

"Not today, I'm afraid," Sheridan said, "We have much to be getting on with, though I do owe you a pint, and make no mistake!"

"I'll hold you to that. I'm rarely out of the Maiden's Arms these days," the Duke grinned, shaking Sheridan's hand.

He knelt before Letisha and took her hand in his. "Until we meet again, Letisha."

*

Sheridan and Letisha sat on the edge of the fountain to eat the picnic Uncle Sigmund had provided.

"If I had known you'd get dragged away like that, I wouldn't have come today," Sheridan confessed. "I only wanted to show you Gram-Shank while you were here."

"It's alright," she crunched through an apple. "We don't have to tell Uncle Sigmund everything. Now, tell me about Selena."

"If I had to describe her politely," he said, "I would say she is nothing short of cold and terrifying, with eyes as piercing as a banshee's cry. I'll admit I was trying to put off going to Tempera-Sleus."

"Funny," Letisha said, petting the clock as it quivered in her bag. "I'd imagine Selena to be quite beautiful. Wasn't Selena a Greek goddess? We learned about it at school…"

"She is dark and secretive, and doesn't put up with the Oddfolk unless she needs something only they can provide."

"But isn't she just like the Oddfolk?"

"She is an enchantress; one with the land around her. She has lived a long time and will continue to do so as long as the land does. Don't be taken in by appearances. Just as I look frightening but am not, Selena is not what she seems. She will see straight through you if you let her."

Letisha did not mention that she knew exactly who Selena was, and that she really didn't seem as bad Sheridan made out. It was as if he expected her to be scared of everything, but the more she thought about the way she and Selena had spoken, the more she could not bring herself to believe that the Enchantress had caused so much damage. Not only that, why didn't she just pick up Letisha and shake an answer out of her if she was so terrifying?

"You're asking a lot of questions," Sheridan said. "Is there something you're not telling me?"

"Always ask questions," Letisha told him, as he had told her the day before. Sheridan smiled. "That's how we learn."

*

Aunt Stackhouse had not stopped complaining for what felt like an eternity. Her throat was sore, but it was not stopping her.

"You let me go this second or I'll have you for assault and attempted murder. I'm a pillar of the community, I'll have you know!"
Her captor was silent, though she heard him moving around, the air freezing whenever he drew near. His breathing was low and almost laboured, as if each lungful was painful.

"You let me go right now, or else…" Aunt Stackhouse began, but stopped mid-sentence, as an icy finger touched her throat, and her voice suddenly ceased. A frosty voice as hard as grit under a tyre spoke:

"I can't stand a woman who lacks the ability to hold her tongue."

Mr Tempus was still blindfolded as he heard the exchange, powerless as he tried to decipher any familiarity in the voice. Suddenly, the sound of platter on stone clattered near him. He felt with his chained hands to find a dish containing lukewarm soup had been pushed through the bars.

"I suppose I should thank you," he muttered, "But I can't eat with my hands bound like this."
He heard the provider of the soup sigh, before his chains crumbled away and hit the floor with a crack. Starving, Mr Tempus wasted no time in drinking down the foul soup. He did not bother to discard his blindfold.

"Where am I? And what did you just do to that woman?" he spluttered through his meal.
His captor breathed heavily, contemplating his reply. Mr Tempus felt a little less drowsy after eating, but had been given an almighty bash on the head and was still suffering. He removed the blindfold, but his captor had already shrunk back into the shadows, and the woman was in darkness. Only her feet could be seen, and Mr Tempus's heart sank as he realised who she was.

"She's of no concern to you. You are in The Fortress of Malice," the captor answered at last, almost out of breath. "But I wouldn't let it concern you."

"Oh?"

"It doesn't matter where you are; you won't be leaving anytime soon."

17

THE ENCHANTRESS OF TEMPURA-SLEUS

Tempera-Sleus sat crouched in the lap of a mountain range, formed of several rocky crags that sprouted from the earth at all angles. Eerily twisted fallen trees continued to grow with their roots exposed, odd, discordant shapes silhouetted against the slate coloured sky. Moss covered the rocky surfaces, glittering with frost as the night drew in. there were no houses, no inhabitants to be seen. The silence was perforated only by the whispering wind. With the lights of Gram-Shank fading far behind them, Letisha wished for the warmth and comfort of home.

"Do you think anyone will notice I'm missing?" she asked Sheridan.

"I shouldn't think so. Time is so distorted here you may well only have been gone for half an hour in your world."

"Really?"

"Or it could be years. I don't really know how these things work." Sheridan admitted.

Letisha frowned, unsettled. "I'm going to get in a lot of trouble if I go home without Mr Tempus."

"Don't worry," said Sheridan, as they began to drop lower. "If Uncle believes in Selena, then so do I."

"How do you know where you're going?" Letisha's voice quavered in the silence of the night. They had only spent an hour in Gram-Shank and already night was firmly upon them.

"I use landmarks wherever I can," he explained. "I could get from Bin Rist to your world with my eyes closed."

They landed in the mouth of a huge, ivy-covered cave. The vines were as thick as Letisha's arms, the leaves forming an emerald curtain. She blinked as she saw lights dancing behind.

"What now?" she whispered, unnerved as her voice made no echo.

A voice interrupted. "Who dares enter the forbidden realm of Tempera-Sleus?"

Both Sheridan and Letisha fell silent. The voice filled the cavern and appeared to have control over who was important enough to echo. Sheridan coughed nervously.

"I have no time for the foolishness of the Oddfolk!" boomed the voice.

Sheridan trembled. Letisha on the other hand was sick of wasting time.

"Please, you're frightening my friend," she patted Sheridan's quivering hand.

"All will cower before the Enchantress of Tempera-Sleus!"

"I'm not scared of a loud voice," Letisha frowned. "It's me; Letisha. I come on business from Bin Rist."

"You've met her before?" Sheridan managed.

The voice was silent. The lights dimmed slightly before the vines unwound and seeped back into cracks in the stone. Behind them sat an enormous eye, whose iris melted from green to gold to blue.

Sheridan shrieked, placed a claw to his forehead and promptly fainted. Letisha and the little clock quivering at her ankles were almost crushed.

"Oh, blast," said the voice, still vibrating the walls. The giant eye began to shrink, and another became visible, and a pretty little nose, full pink lips and a gentle face. Before Letisha could blink Selena stood before her, her silvery hair dazzling in the moonlight.

"Do forgive me, I should have known it would be all too much for Sheridan. He never could stand a fright." She grabbed him under the arms and prepared to heave him through the opening and into the void beyond. Her strength was unbelievable. When Letisha failed to move, the enchantress called back.

"Are you coming in or what?"

Letisha followed obediently into the blackness, guided by Selena's faint blue glow. An earthy odour told her that they were going deep underground.

After an eternity of descent, the tunnel began to flatten out. Selena's glow disappeared against the light of a cavern ahead of them.

Letisha gasped, looking out onto an enormous turquoise lake, reflecting a remarkably starry sky. As she looked up she realised that they were no longer inside, but standing on the sheer edge of a slate rock face. The ledge jutted out over a steep drop below, where a vast forest flourished. Trees of all shapes and sizes swayed in a gentle breeze. Exotic birds flitted in and out. Letisha had a clear view of everything from where they stood, and saw that the floor was covered in young, sweet smelling grass. For a few seconds she almost forgot that they were underground at all.

Sheridan's eyes flickered open, whereupon he made a short shriek as he spotted the enchantress, and promptly swooned again. Letisha tried not to feel embarrassed, unable to resist meeting Selena's gaze. They rolled their eyes together.

Selena knelt and patted Sheridan's cheek in an attempt to bring him round.

"Oh, for goodness' sake," she muttered. As she held out her gloved hand a small glowing orb appeared, hovering above her palm. She waved it under Sheridan's nose. His eyes rolled open.

"Oh glory, the delicious orb!" he said weakly.

As soon as she was certain that he was awake, Selena snatched the orb away. She placed it atop a staff resembling a stag's antler that had appeared out of nowhere just as the orb had.

"Do get up, Sheridan," said Selena. "What would your uncle say if he saw you rolling about on the floor like that?"

"Terribly sorry," he stood and dusted himself off.

Selena nodded and turned to Letisha.

"I expected it was only a matter of time before you gave in to temptation and strayed through that blasted portal. A mortal in Tempera-Sleus," she chuckled to herself. "That's a new one. I've been expecting you."

"You have?"

"What kind of person would I be if I didn't keep an eye on you once you dared to wander through? There are dark forces at work and I didn't want anyone else to get a hold of you first."

"Well you needn't have made such a fuss about letting us in," Sheridan fanned himself with his hand, as if he might faint again.

"Sheridan!" Letisha hissed, before she lowered her eyes and said, "I suppose I didn't really think about it. I'm more concerned with finding Mr Tempus."

Selena indicated that they should both follow her down a set of steep slate stairs that carved themselves into the cliff face as they descended, the orb lighting their way.

Selena took them to the reflecting pool, where a set of stone chairs and a matching table sat, glistening in the moonlight. She raised her free hand and another dozen orbs rose from the ground and lit the area. Selena invited her guests to sit with her. As soon as they sat down, Letisha found that she could not stop the story from pouring out of her in every detail, including how she had found Sheridan singing in the wrecked stock room.

Selena leaned on her hands and nodded in interest, as her face grew more concerned.

"You are both tired, and you're not going anywhere in the dark. Let me fetch some refreshments, and we'll see what's to be done," she said suddenly.

"But…" Letisha began, unable to stifle a yawn. Sheridan yawned too, his mouth as wide as a crocodiles'. He laid his head on his arms and closed his eyes. Letisha found the uncontrollable urge to sleep surrounding her, so she followed him.

Quietly, Selena slipped away.

Letisha awoke to the little clock prodding at her face with its bells. She sat up, rubbing her eyes. The forest was dark and silent, the orbs dimmed to a gentle moonlight glow. She felt that they were not longer alone, grimacing as she recognised the voice that stirred her.

"Sleeping at the table? What a foul-mannered toad you are."
Letisha looked around and tried to spot Mrs Grisham's Ghost. Amongst the orbs, she would be easy to miss.

"Hello, Mrs Grisham's Ghost," she said politely. "What brings you to Tempera-Sleus?"

"None of your business!"
The ghost materialised beside Sheridan, still sleeping soundly. She looked particularly disgruntled, and seemed to have brought the cold night air inside with her.

"Disgusting, stupid creature." She glared at the dragon slumped over the table. What's it doing here?"

"He's not disgusting or stupid," Letisha snapped. "He's my friend."
Ignoring the ghost, she nudged Sheridan to wake him.

"No more bird soup, thank you uncle," he muttered in his sleep.

"Sheridan" Letisha hissed. "Wake up!"

Sheridan opened one yellow eye. "Is it time to go?"

"I don't think it's morning yet," Letisha concluded as she stood up. "I can't see Selena anywhere."

Sheridan sat up properly. "I want to go home; she hasn't helped us at all. Here's an idea," he rubbed his hands together. "I bet the Ouroboros could make it morning, and we could go." He noticed Mrs Grisham's Ghost standing beside him, scowling as if sucking a lemon. "Ah, the spirit!"

The ghost ignored him and turned to Letisha. "What's he prattling about?"

"It's not ours to play with," Letisha said sternly to Sheridan. She couldn't resist the urge to take the Ouroboros out of her bag. It was still warm in her hand. "It doesn't look like much, does it?"

"Never judge a book by its cover," said Mrs Grisham's Ghost. "I believe my late husband owned one of those. Very expensive, but he could afford it…"

Sheridan cut in before she could begin her life story, and took the watch. "See the stones?" He said, indicating the three crystals set into the golden case, framed by an ornate swirl engraved into the metal. "They represent the three Architects, blue for Frost, green for Earth, and red for Time. Fascinating." He popped the watch open to the second face. The green liquid bubbled in anticipation.

"Don't do anything stupid," Letisha warned. "We'll get into trouble."

"Don't get it dirty!" cried the ghost. "When was the last time you washed those grubby paws?"

"I'm not going to do anything," Sheridan reassured her, and flipped to the third face. "Letisha! One of the pawn cogs has your name on it now! How did that happen?"

"Let me see!" Letisha excitedly snatched the watch, her fingers mashing the cogs as she did so. She suddenly felt very warm, as a green haze surrounded her where she sat. It started at her feet and swirled up her body like a smoky serpent. The room was disappearing from her vision as the haze thickened. She felt as if her skin was shrinking and her muscles were not. It was more uncomfortable than painful, though she felt dizzy. The Ouroboros suddenly became enormous in her hands. "What happened?" she squeaked.

Sheridan shrieked. "You activated the Ouroboros! Look at you, you're so cute!"

Letisha closed the Ouroboros and looked at herself in the polished surface. Her clothes were too big and her face had grown rounder. One of her boots flopped off her foot onto the floor.

"It shrunk me!" she cried.

"It made you younger!" Sheridan clapped his hands excitedly. Letisha stood up with some difficulty, as she was now quite a lot shorter than she had been and had to jump down from the chair. She retrieved her boot and tried to tie the laces, but found she could not. Sheridan now loomed over her more than he had done before.

Sheridan giggled. "You're like a little doll!"

"An even smaller, more insolent madam." Mrs Grisham's Ghost grumbled.

"Stop it!" Letisha snapped. "How do I undo it? Where's the book?" She reached for her bag and pulled out the book, weighing a ton in her tiny arms. She flicked to the marked page of the Ouroboros, where the dials and cogs were explained, though not terribly clearly. She could see the cog with her name on it was described as a Pawn Cog, or at least those around the edge were. Her name was on the central cog, but in her panic she made little sense of any of it.

"I can't understand all the big words!" she shrieked.

"Stupid as well as insolent!" Mrs Grisham's Ghost piped up. "Will you just look at yourself?"

Letisha rushed to the reflective pool behind them, where she saw herself clearly. Her clothes now swamped her, as did her mane of unkempt hair, which was even messier after all the flying. Her cheeks were chubbier and her eyes were red from crying.

"I can't be more than five years old! I can't go back to school like this!" She began to cry again.

Heartbroken and trying not to cry himself, Sheridan wrung his tail in his hands.

"Oh, it's not so bad," he tried to comfort her. "Just think of all the lovely little outfits that will fit you again, and...and...blast, what do little girls like?"

"Do be quiet," said Mrs Grisham's Ghost. She had no idea how to comfort a crying child. There was almost a pang of sympathy in her voice. "Come no, crying never solved anything, did it?"

Letisha howled even as she tried to stop herself, until a sharp metallic noise reverberated around the cavern. A blue light proceeded Selena, who roared.

"What is going on here?"

Both Letisha and Sheridan were silent. Mrs Grisham's Ghost promptly evaporated. Selena carried a silver tray holding three crystal glasses, quivering as she shook, Her face drained of colour, her eyes glowered

"There is something you have not told me," she said sharply. "It will do no good keeping secrets."

still had tears pouring down her five year old cheeks.

"Child, you will come with me." Selena said. "Dragon, you stay here and keep your hands to yourself."

Selena led Letisha away from the cavern in silence. Fear curdled her stomach and stuck in her throat like a boiled sweet as the gravity of the situation hit her.

Looking back over her shoulder she saw Sheridan biting his claws and clutching the book for comfort. The little clock anxiously hopped up and down on the table.

The lights in the cavern had dimmed once more as the enchantress calmed herself, although Letisha could still feel the tension cracking in the air like static electricity. She still carried the Ouroboros. It was tremendously heavy, almost breathing in her hands. It felt as though it had been awoken after a long sleep.

18

THE NIXIES OF MALICE

Half mad with hunger, Aunt Stackhouse opened her eyes and attempted to take in her surroundings. The walls were made of what she took for dirty, faded marble. The room was huge but she was being held in a small alcove. She was shackled at the ankles and the wrists, barely able to move. A bowl of icy water sat just inside the bars that held her.

She was still angry and unable to speak; her tongue and lips were frozen so that she could only drink. She was weak from not eating, but her stubbornness burned. Across the cell she saw another prisoner, though he was obscured by darkness. She was certain that Mr Tempus lay sleeping across from her, but she couldn't be sure. The whole situation was utter madness. She could not speak to him, but assumed he would be of little use anyway. She was unsure of how long she had been a prisoner for or who had taken her, but she blamed Mr Tempus.

Outside she heard the chattering of the little creatures that guarded her, though. She kicked the bars as they came closer, making them jump and giggle.

Vile little things, she thought. Let me out of here and I'll give you something to giggle about!

She unreservedly regretted her foolish pursuit of Letisha Tate. If she did escape, she decided, she would take great pleasure in telling her dear sister and brother-in-law that their precious misfit had vanished into thin air.

Suddenly, the little creatures stopped their noise and shrank a little. The one who had frozen her tongue spoke to them in a whisper. In the pit of her bitter little stomach, she felt a stab of fear.

A face obscured by a hood came down to her level. Though she only saw his chin and the lower half of his mouth, she could tell it was a sharp, pointed face with a spiteful tongue and icy eyes. A shudder ran through her even as she imagined his form.

Coldness crept from his dry lips as he spoke to her, though she had missed his question.

Aunt Stackhouse frowned.

"Oh, silly me. I made you hold your tongue, didn't I?"

A gust of cold, slightly stagnant breath left his mouth, and suddenly Aunt Stackhouse felt her tongue loosen.

"You let me out of here, or else," she crowed at him.

"Or else I take your tongue again?" he said smugly. "I was just saying to my nixies, bringing me a gruff middle aged hag is a bit different to bringing me the small mortal girl I asked for. Wouldn't you agree?"

"How dare you!" said Aunt Stackhouse. "And what do you mean, mortal girl?"

"There was a girl residing behind that portal. What was her name?"

Aunt Stackhouse felt a twinge of humanity. "I don't know." She shouted in pain as the shackles around her ankles tightened.

"You're nothing to do with this, my good woman. Pray, tell me your name."

"Miss Stackhouse," she said shortly, thinking she could change the subject.

"Miss? Now there's a surprise," he smirked. "You may call me Jack."

"I'd rather call you something else," she said.

"Miss Stackhouse." Jack said sternly. "Tell me where she is. No harm will come to her, only she has something very precious to me, and I would hate to see it broken or misused. Little girls can be careless, can't they?"

Aunt Stackhouse thought; Letisha was clumsy, and if she damaged something somebody would have to pay for it. His voice was as smooth as ice.

"I don't know where she is," she admitted. "Letisha wasn't in the shop so far as I could see..."

"As we suspected," Jack rubbed his thin, sickly hands together. "There you have it, my nixies; our young friend must be in our world now. No doubt she will be easy to find."

Aunt Stackhouse could say nothing else. He was gone and out the door before she even had a chance to beg for something to eat.

*

Letisha followed the enchantress along a path into the trees. Above them the ceiling of the chasm was no longer full of stars, but black and flat as the slate that formed the cliff face. Once again it felt as though they were inside. Letisha was having trouble adjusting to being so much shorter. Her clothes were hanging off her and her boots thudded awkwardly as she scuttled along. Selena walked ahead in silence, her staff beating against the floor. The trees thinned out as the cavern began to narrow into a tunnel. Before long, they were in darkness, led only by Selena's faint glow. As the tunnel enveloped them, the air became warmer. The heat caught in Letisha's throat and made her thankful for her coat's looseness.

"I don't care for the cold," Selena stated, as if she heard Letisha's thoughts. "And I find most things grow better with a little heat."
Letisha realised that the tunnel's walls were not so much lined with roots, but made from roots. They intertwined with one another, some sprouting leaves, others with the fine white beginnings of yet more roots. They grew at an impossible rate, the smaller vines thickening and lengthening within seconds of first sprouting. Looking back Letisha was alarmed to see that the tunnel was closing off behind them, knitting together into a solid wooden mass.

"We're going to be trapped," she squeaked, drawing closer to the enchantress for comfort.

"Poor girl. Playing with the Ouroboros has its consequences. I believe you were always in the wrong order, but this has really thrown a spanner in the works."

"I beg your pardon, but how can I be in the wrong order?" Letisha asked.

"The question is how now can you ever be in the right order if you are too small for all your components?"
Letisha had no answer. Riddles weren't her specialty.
Selena banged her staff against the floor, and the light disappeared. Letisha reminded herself that she had given up being afraid of the dark when she was eight, and her fear was misguided. Having the drives and fears of a five year old, but the reasoning and common sense of a scatter-brained eleven year old was a confusing place. In her heart she did not want to be afraid of Selena, since she came so highly recommended by Uncle Sigmund. She had also claimed to be a friend of Mr Tempus, though they seemed to be estranged. Being little again was making her afraid of nearly everything, but in this case she knew she had angered Selena, and had foolishly left Sheridan behind.
Selena struck the floor again and the tunnel was illuminated, except it wasn't a tunnel any longer, but another huge chamber formed entirely of plant-matter. Newer roots replaced older ones, the walls slowly undulating with life.
Selena held out her hand, and Letisha could not control the urge to pass the Ouroboros to her. It was as if a force bigger than anything she could comprehend wrapped itself around her and insisted that it was the right thing to do.
The enchantress tilted the watch in her fingertips, letting the light dance on its surface.

"Mortals should not use the Ouroboros. I am surprised you managed to work such magic on yourself. How did you do it?"

"I don't know," Letisha admitted. "My fingers must have turned one of the cogs by accident. I took it from Sheridan after he said one of the scrolls had my name on it. Mr Tempus gave me a book that told us all about it."

"He gave you Classic Collectible Timepieces?" she said, as if recalling a distant memory. "You've certainly done your homework, haven't you? What else has he taught you?"

"Not much," Letisha muttered, her chin in her collar. "I can put a few bits together, but nothing like the workings of an Ouroboros. According to Mr Tempus, it's only a thing of myth. That's why we suspected he'd been taken, because a mortal shouldn't own an Ouroboros, should he?"

"Indeed," Selena mused, almost disappointed that Letisha hadn't learned more. "It seems odd that even the person in control is still described as a pawn, doesn't it?"

"Mr Tempus says that we all affect one another's' actions, just like the cogs in a watch," Letisha recalled.

Selena smiled as she opened the watch and showed it to Letisha. As before, in the central cog, Letisha's name was engraved clear as day.

"Now, can you perhaps tell me how this happened?"

Letisha shook her head sulkily

"I know who this Ouroboros should belong to, but it seems that it has temporarily chosen you to be its guardian."

"But Sheridan has been taking care of it, not me."

"He hasn't been carrying it around with him, has he?"

"No, it's been locked away safe before now."

"Well there we are then." Selena paused, and lowered her eyes. "This isn't really Sigmund Adelinda's business, is it? And Letisha, do be honest with me."

Letisha shook her head.

"But it isn't exactly yours, either. I think perhaps there is another force at work here."

"Mr Tempus is in trouble," said Letisha. "And we think it's because of this thing. He was kidnapped, and the stockroom torn apart. I thought perhaps you might have come back and lost your temper…"

Selena raised her eyebrows, and for a moment genuine concern shattered her cool demeanour.

"That really isn't my style. But I'm glad you didn't come here pointing the finger."

"Nobody knows I met you already," Letisha admitted. "I think Sheridan has an idea by now, but I told you I could keep a promise. I've told you everything I know."

Selena smiled as she lowered her eyes. "I am an enchantress, my dear. I saw you and the dragon coming a mile off. But there are things you're not telling me."

"I made a promise," Letisha maintained. "What happens in the Watch Room stays in the Watch Room."

Before she could breathe another word, the roots began to morph. Wild wood snapped into rigid rows; the floor went from damp slate to polished wood; the cavernous atmosphere gave way to high ceilings and distant windows, filtering in weak sunlight. Turning a circle, Letisha recognised the Watch Room, covered in dust and forgotten, as it had been before.

"Well, now we are in the Watch Room. I think I have held up my half. Now," Selena said smugly. She knelt down so she was face to face with five-year-old Letisha. "Spill it."

Letisha welled up again, and couldn't believe what a cry-baby she had been. She still didn't want to break her promise, but felt she had no choice.

"He told me about his duties as Father Time," she sighed as the weight of the secret lifted off her, "I only found out by accident. But he had given the Ouroboros to Sheridan for safekeeping, so he must have known it was valuable and that somebody wanted it. I think he saw it in the book and just put two and two together. From what Uncle Sigmund said, I think he is one of three somethings,"

"Architects," Selena said, examining the Ouroboros as if it were a long lost friend whose name she was trying to remember. "There was a time when Mr Tempus was really quite ordinary. He had a wife and a son, and a little business that did well. Such was his talent for the craft of watches that people would travel for miles to that sleepy little village to have their timepieces fixed and cleaned, or indeed to commission special projects. When do you think this would have been?"

"He couldn't tell me how old he was," Letisha admitted.

"I'm not sure myself," said the enchantress. "Age means very little to me, but all I know is that his happiness was not to last. He lost his wife; disease could appear out of nowhere and it killed quickly in those days. Not long after that, his son also fell ill too.

"His prayers were answered when a man named Father Time stepped forward to offer a solution. 'Do my work for just a little while, and you shall have your son restored to you in good health', he said."

"But it hasn't been a little while," Letisha interrupted.

"He gave Mr Tempus the Watch Room, and access to the portal so that he might pop in from time to time. And he took his son away, as assurance that Mr Tempus would serve him dutifully, until the debt was repaid." Selena paused, still examining the Ouroboros. "Do you suppose Mr Tempus likes what he does?"

Letisha shook her head. "I think he is tired."

"Mr Tempus fell in love with the wrong woman. His wife was so much more than she appeared, and there is a reason for Father Time's behaviour. Did Sigmund tell you about the other Architects?"

"Not really, he told me that Father Time accused Mother Earth of living a separate life with a mortal man...." Letisha raised her eyebrows. Selena smiled wryly. "Mr Tempus?"

"Indeed. The job of Father Time is a lonely one now. He punished Mother Earth for leaving him, slaying her mortal body and leaving her as little more than an entity. He punished the man she loved by stealing away his son and then promising his return for a price."

"I don't think I like Father Time," Letisha admitted.

"They do say that Time makes fools of us all," Selena sighed. "Mr Tempus just got caught in the wrong place at the wrong time."

"But surely if Mother Earth loved him, she could do something?"

"Father Time is powerful. Mr Tempus barely remembers his wife, as you'll have noticed. This was a punishment for them both. She was bound to stay in the Otherworld by dark magic too powerful for her to combat; death, if only mortal death, weakened her sufficiently. It would be a risk for her to come too close to Mr Tempus.

"He has spent too long on his own. I imagine you were welcomed very warmly."

"He's kind," Letisha agreed. "And he doesn't treat me like I'm stupid."

"You aren't stupid, Letisha," Selena's face softened slightly. "But you are in danger, and I have already told you too much."

19

THE TICKERS DESCEND

In the main cavern, Sheridan seated himself back at the table, and flicked distractedly through the book. He leaned his head on his hand and decided that he was too worried about Letisha to dribble over the watches. He had cooked and eaten his eels, toasting them with one fiery breath. Somewhere in the shadows the ghost still lurked, waiting to poke her nose into their business.

Sheridan's left ear twitched. He could no longer hear the voices of Letisha and Selena. They were far away, concealed by her enchantment. He could hear other voices, though; little chattering voices, approaching fast from the cave through which they had entered.

"Do you hear…?" Sheridan began to the ghost, just as the vines concealing the entrance were slashed violently from the other side, and the cavern filled with air so cold the dragon's eyes watered. The leaves of the trees withered and the patter of large, flat feet on the slate grew louder. Before Sheridan could even think, a horde of what he recognised as nixies was making its way towards him, squealing gleefully as they chopped their way through the trees. They were no bigger than children, only three or four feet tall. They had spiteful little faces with sharp lips and small eyes. Twitching, bat-like ears listened for movement. They had just about reached the clearing, when Sheridan felt a cold hand on each shoulder.

"Grab the satchel."

As he followed the ghost's orders, she wrapped her smoky arms around him and evaporated in a cloud of blue-grey smoke. Sheridan found that he could see the horde perfectly, but they could not see him.

The ghost hissed in his ear. "If you speak, they will see you. Letisha is in trouble."

Sheridan raised his horned eyebrows.

"Get out if you can," hissed Mrs Grisham's Ghost. "I can get the bag to Letisha, wherever the witch sends her."

Sheridan shook his head, insistent that he would not leave Letisha. Around them, the nixies were destroying everything.

Sheridan knew he would stand little chance against so many. They were all armed in one way or another, with clubs, knives or daggers. One even had an impressive antique musket hanging from her belt.

"Go now!" hissed the ghost.

"No, I won't leave her!" Sheridan cried, then clasped his hands to his mouth. With an exasperated shriek the ghost disintegrated, along with the satchel. Sheridan was now visible. Unable to see any other option, he flapped his great wings and took off vertically, knocking a dozen nixies to the floor with his great tail. They squawked and hurled whatever missiles they had.

  Sheridan squeezed his eyes closed and continued to flap. He waited for the bump to his head, but was unable to reach the ceiling. As the air grew colder and his ears popped, he realised he was much higher than expected.

Sheridan opened his eyes to the darkness of night-time. Below him, where there should have been Selena's hollow, he saw only the tops of trees. The cavern was now inaccessible, and Letisha was lost.

*

"You must go quickly," Selena told Letisha, as blue lights flashed and whispered behind the roots. The enchantress seemed to understand their message. She looked around, from one orb to another, her eyes alight with the formation of ideas.

She seized the Ouroboros from her pocket and set about fiddling with the cogs, until a green bolt of lightning shot from its face and surrounded Letisha. She felt her feet stretch to fill her shoes, and the fabric of the coat shrink across her shoulders. She was nearer her own age, but still not quite there. She was about seven years old. She had grown a lot between five and seven, but she was still comparatively short.

"This isn't right," cried Letisha. "I was older than this!"

"It will have to do for now," said the enchantress. "They know you are here."

"Who?"

"The nixies."

Selena swept her hands across the wall, parting the roots to reveal open air on the other side of her hideaway. Letisha could see the snow-capped mountains under a starry sky.

"The Blue Mountains," Selena explained. "If I set you down here you can get away."

She gently pushed Letisha towards the opening, where the cold struck and made her eyes water. Steps were cut into the steep rock face before her, as the ancient trees dotted on either side leaned courteously out of their way, reaching into the sky and almost disappearing from sight.

"What about Sheridan? And what's a nixie?" Letisha asked. She was reluctant to leave and baffled as to why Selena would desert her in the middle of nowhere

"Something you don't want to tangle with. They're the minions of Jack Frost, and if they catch you you'll end up in Malice," said Selena. "I only hope Time doesn't send the tickers after you as well."

"What?" Letisha didn't like the sound of that. "What on earth is a ticker?"

"You'll know the tickers are on to you if you hear them," Selena said quickly, as if she hoped Letisha would not encounter either of these pests. "Make your way back to the other side of the mountains, it won't take you more than half an hour's flight; Sheridan will already be looking for you. Go quickly."

"What, where?"

"Somewhere safe… go back to Gram-Shank," she said confidently. Letisha was not sure if she had even told Selena that they had been to Gram-Shank. "Go to the inn; there is somebody there who can help you."

"What about you?" Letisha tried to keep the irritation out of her voice. "Can you do nothing to help us?"

"I will work faster on my own, and you will be safe with Sheridan. Now go!"

With a push, Selena sent her skittering down the stairs with more force than perhaps intended. Letisha began to feel gravity working against her tired little legs. Exhaustion had made her dizzy, as well as being so much closer to the ground. Before she could stop herself, Letisha began to tumble. Her stomach leaped into her throat as the world turned upside down.
Her knee clipped the edge of a particularly sharp step sending white-hot pain up and down her leg. She was rolling uncontrollably towards an expanse of water below her in the darkness.
She shot off the last step and onto the surface of the frozen river that cut its way between the crags with a thud. She lay face down on the ice, groaning. Her whole body ached. She remembered that if she spread out her weight the ice was less likely to crack and commit her to the depths of the water.
In the sudden quiet of the chill evening, she closed her eyes tight shut in frustration, as she realised that she had lost her bag. She had also lost Sheridan, and even the minimal help of Mrs Grisham's Ghost. She was being pursued by something she knew nothing about. She had a long trek ahead of her to a town full of characters that might try to marinate and eat her. And to make matters worse she heard the distinctive cracking of ice.

Letisha barely had time to scream before she was plunged into the water, so cold it took her breath away as though she had been punched in the stomach. The water was pitch-black; she could no longer tell which way was up. Even as she struggled under the weight of the water thinking she was done for, she felt a hand grab the collar of her coat and haul her from the jaws of doom. She coughed and spluttered atop the ice.

Letisha pulled the sopping hair from her eyes and coughed up river water. Shivering, she looked around to see that her saviour was not Sheridan as she hoped, but a pretty young woman with dark hair and pale skin. She wore rough peasant clothes, but had a kind face. She was tiny, barely past Letisha's shoulder. Letisha was still in shock as she looked around and realised that they were not alone; at least a dozen more young women gathered round, chattering amongst themselves in a strange language. They were very excited.

"Poor thing," said the first girl. "Are you alright?"

"I'm fine," Letisha lied, tattered, freezing and concussed. She tried to stand up but her cut knee refused to let her. "Who are you?"

"We are friends of the enchantress," explained the first girl. "She told us of your escape, so we came to help." With unnatural strength, she lifted Letisha to her feet and handed her hat back, lost during her fall. Another girl put a blanket around her shoulders.

Letisha clutched it around her, then realised that they were still standing on thin ice. She looked around and realised that the hole through which she had fallen was gone. The girls clustered around her, making Letisha feel a little uneasy. Were there more than before?

"Well, thank you for your help, but I have a long journey ahead of me," she shivered.

"You should travel by river, like us" said the first girl, and began to skate around in a perfect figure of eight. "It's the only way to travel."

"I'd rather walk." Letisha began to limp to the edge of the water. Her knee was throbbing and she was certain the graze would begin sticking to her tights.

"Oh, no! Have a go!" One of the girls dragged her back by her arm. She skated backwards, holding Letisha's arms so she was being pulled forwards. She had dropped her blanket, but it was panic that pricked her skin rather than the icy air.

The girls were skating faster, moving Letisha up river and away from the pass through the mountains she was headed for. Despite her suspicions, she decided to play their games until they got bored, lest they become angry and leave her to an icy grave. She was already shivering violently, her wet hair slick and freezing down her back.

What did concern her was how well they skated, even though they wore no skates, or even shoes for that matter. They moved while barely touching the ice, almost blue with cold.

Suddenly, a roar shattered the evening as a dark shape with a shimmering belly approached. The girls stopped in their tracks, hissing as Letisha felt dozens of strong hands holding onto her arms and shoulders. Sharp, impossibly cold nails dug into her skin. The shape drew closer, launching a huge fireball towards them. The girls gave an ear piercing scream, dispersed and left her alone.

As the flames died down, there was a mighty snap as the ice became thin under Letisha's feet.

"Don't just stand there, get on, quick!"

Letisha dived onto Sheridan's back and they rocketed off into the night sky, the wind roaring in her ears and whipping her sodden hair behind her. Letisha despondently saw the girls reappear. Their pleasant faces had become pinched and ugly, their hair wild and flailing. They were no longer pretty, but monstrous mishaps, screeching furiously.

Sheridan doubled back and dropped lower, hurling another fireball. The river melted in an instant, sending the creatures squawking. They dripped as they ran, shrinking like melting icicles.

When Sheridan was satisfied that all the creatures were gone, he gained altitude once more. Letisha gripped his scarf and wrapped her legs around him tightly, before she asked,

"What were those things?"

"Nixies," Sheridan wheezed.

"Ah."

"They ambushed us in the cavern but I managed to escape. I've been looking for you. What happened?"

"I fell through the ice," Letisha explained. "They rescued me, but they wouldn't let me go."

"I dare say they caused the accident," said Sheridan. "Everyone knows that the River Airvia never freezes, not without help from certain disagreeable creatures…."

Sheridan cut off, swaying violently as a blow struck his head. Another hit his side, and Letisha realised that they were being pelted with enormous hailstones. One hit his left wing, making him sway abruptly to one side. Somehow he caught himself and soldiered on, even as he puffed for breath.

Just as she felt that they might escape, Letisha heard something that made Selena's words echo in her mind; 'you'll know the tickers are on you when you hear them.'

From left and right, a swarm of insects was closing around them, an insane ticking emitting from their wings. Letisha briefly thought of the sound of the little shop, and how differently these pests sounded. Shrieking, she batted an enormous beetle from her arm. Its wings shimmered like glass, hidden away beneath a copper shell. It ticked as it flew and joined the swarm, which continued to close in. On seeing a few more up close, Letisha was surprised to see how much the creatures actually looked like tiny pocket watches, their cases splitting like wings, beating together to form a terrible chorus of ticking. She recognised it as the same sound that preceded Mr Dreamseller outside the little shop.

"Sheridan!" she cried, "Tickers!"

Sheridan beat his wings as fast as he could manage, as hailstones and tickers alike hindered him. "Let's see if these little beasties can fly as fast as a dragon!"

Letisha gripped the scarf white-knuckled, her eyes streaming from the biting wind. Tickers crawled through her hair and even inside her coat. It was a truly disgusting feeling and she prayed they didn't bite.

Sheridan was also covered from head to toe in the shimmering insects, weighing him down. Even as he fought to gain altitude, a nixie with a good arm managed to hit him in the side of the head with a mammoth hailstone. Letisha saw his eyes roll back as he was knocked unconscious.

They began to plummet.

20

TRAVELLING BY DREAM

Letisha shook Sheridan and begged him to wake as she felt certain the end in sight. The wind roared as the ground drew up faster than she could fathom. Sheridan awoke and snapped out his wings just in time to catch them from being dashed to pieces on the floor of the valley. Instead, his body halted suddenly, where he found they were caught in a net a few feet from the ground. Dazed, Letisha rolled off the dragons back and into the surrounding greenery. She started as an icy hand clamped over her mouth, indicating that she should stay silent.

The net that held Sheridan was suspended from four pillars of ice, which melted into four nixies. They moved in quickly, tying the net at the top to prevent his escape. Sheridan's frightened eyes flickered as the nixies hauled him along the ground, made smooth with a flawless coating of ice.
With Sheridan captured, the swarm of tickers dispersed, leaving the night in silence, save for the low chattering of the nixies as they walked.

Letisha froze as an icy palm clamped over her mouth. She saw Sheridan's hopeless expression as the nixies dragged him away up the river. He said nothing, and simply let them take him. Her heart sank and fear returned. She might have lost the nixies, but she had also lost Sheridan, possibly for good if she imagined the worst.

Letisha tore the freezing hand away and turned to find the face of Mrs Grisham's Ghost inches from her own. Frantically she patted herself down and shook her body, hoping to get rid of any remaining tickers. A single one fell from her sleeve and attempted to scuttle away. Letisha stamped on it so hard her ankle throbbed. Lifting her boot, she saw that it had been built, not born. Only a pile of cogs and twisted metal remained.
Incapable of screaming, Letisha whipped her head back to where Sheridan had been.

"Why did you rescue me?" she cried, furious. "Sheridan needed help! Why did you let them take him?"

"Don't you speak to me like that, insolent vixen! I didn't have to rescue anyone!"

"No, you didn't, you stupid old woman!" Letisha snapped. "So why did you?"

Mrs Grisham's Ghost was finally shocked to silence. Sheepishly, she produced the satchel from her smoky robes.

"Sheridan has more of a chance with a gang of nixies than you do. He's bigger and stronger and not nearly so stupid as he seems. Once he regains consciousness he'll fight."

"And me?"

"You have to find Mr Tempus," Mrs Grisham's Ghost corrected herself. "We have to find him."

"But Selena said…"

"She doesn't know what she's talking about. Not to mention she didn't put you back right. If you want something done, do it yourself."

"But…"

"Hush. We need to get you somewhere warm before you end up like me."

"We're miles from anywhere! How am I supposed to get back to Gram-Shank?"

"In your dreams," shrugged the ghost simply.

"What?"

"Pardon."

"I said 'what?'" Letisha returned, confused.

"No, you say 'pardon', not 'what'. Speak nicely."

Letisha rolled her eyes. "Sorry. Pardon?"

"Now you're going off the subject!"

"In my dreams! What are you talking about?!" Letisha's exclamation echoed off the mountains. She clenched her fists at her sides, in both frustration and to combat the biting cold.

A bristling frown cut into the ghosts' brow.

"That little bottle in your bag is tremendously powerful and very valuable. I assume you stole it."

Letisha folded her arms, shivering. "It was given to me by a Dreamseller. And he said it would just give me vivid dreams."

"In your world," said the ghost. "In this world, it is anything you want it to be. Just take a little sip."

Letisha took the tiny bottle from her bag, which had been wedged in between the book and her clock, which appeared to be sleeping.

She looked at the dream suspiciously. There were no instructions, and she doubted the ghost knew what she was talking about. She had little choice, and pulled out the cork before pouring a drop on her tongue. It tasted like pineapples.

"Quickly," urged the ghost. "Just think about where you want to be. And make sure you dream that I'm there too..." her voice began to fade, and Letisha saw a parade of purple spots before her eyes, and all too soon the world disintegrated, and she was herself no longer.

21

JACK

Letisha awoke to a deafening roar. She heard laughing and chattering, and the roar of an enormous fire. From somewhere far off came the sound of a slurred drunken song. As Selena had suggested, she was inside an inn. Letisha only hoped it was the right one.

"I did it!" she whispered in awe.

Not a second after Letisha had found her footing, a white light blossomed beside her, and Mrs Grisham's Ghost appeared. Her face twisted disapprovingly.

"Nasty filthy place. Why have you brought us here?"

Letisha opened her mouth to speak, but had little chance before the ghost snapped, "And don't talk to me, not unless you want to look completely insane." She waved a hand in front of the face of ugly looking ogre-type creature at the bar. He didn't react. "I'm a ghost, remember?"

Letisha nodded and approached the bar. She knew she was too young to be in a pub, and looked even younger. She had no choice, as the ghost wasn't being helpful.

"Could I have a hot drink, please?" She shivered quietly.

Nobody heard her. The boar-like barman, who was easily eight feet tall, ignored her completely and continued showing an ugly scar on his hand to a patron.

"You'll have to do better than that," the ghost scoffed.

"And I suppose you come in a lot of taverns?" Letisha hissed impatiently.

"What do you take me for, a common farm dweller?!" A gust of icy air left her translucent body and shuddered across the room, turning heads as it did. Letisha smiled smugly at the ghost before turning back to the attention of the barman.

"I'd like a hot drink, please," she said.

The boar-man smiled. "Of course, is tea alright? Anyone would think you'd had a run in with a gang of nixies, the state of you!"

"Well actually," she muttered. "I did."

The barman gasped and the room fell silent. Every head in the tavern turned to look her up and down in awe as though she had accomplished some incredible feat. Nobody spoke for a moment, before a murmur turned into excited chatter. The barman placed a steaming mug on the counter.

"Pay for your drink and find a place to dry off," the ghost hissed. "We'll only get hounded if you keep talking."

Letisha did as she was told, breaking off the story with vague details. She placed her bag on the counter to find a few coins Sheridan had given her. The little clock awoke from its sleep, ringing in alarm and bouncing off along the counter as though it was on fire. A few of the patrons looked at Letisha angrily as the clock knocked over their tankards. She paid quickly, with extra to cover the damage, and picked up her mug and bag. She took off to the back of the tavern, grabbing the clock by its bells on the way.

Letisha found a table next to the fire, where she removed her boots and allowed her freezing feet to dry. She hung her coat on the back of the dragon-sized chair. It felt even more enormous as she struggled to become accustomed to the tiny body she now feared she was stuck with. The ghost sat down opposite her.

"You draw too much attention to yourself. It doesn't become a young lady to brag."

"I just nearly froze to death in a river," Letisha frowned, hugging the mug between her hands. "I wasn't bragging."

*

Mr Tempus was dreaming, a welcome escape from the hard icy pillow beneath his head.

He was young again, having just completed his apprenticeship. He was signing the deed to his new shop. A few friends had stopped by for the grand opening. Everyone was full of good cheer, but he wasn't really interested in them; hidden in the crowd was a young woman with red hair wound into a long plait down her back. She had a pale gentle face and dancing green eyes, and wore an ivy coloured dress. She smiled at him and he fell instantly in love.

A few years passed and he was an established watchmaker, with customers travelling far and wide to partake of his excellent services. Life was good, but it was made better by the presence of his new wife, the beautiful Anna, who lived with him in the tiny rooms above the shop. They were soon to be blessed with a child.

Their son Toby was a treasure, just like his mother. Mr Tempus doted on him unconditionally, hoping one day to pass the business onto Toby, whom he knew he could trust with his life's work.

All too quickly things began to change; Anna succumbed to illness and passed away, tearing his heart in two. And now his precious son of twelve was fading too. Mr Tempus prayed that his son would recover, but everything seemed hopeless. He had lost the love of his life and was soon to lose everything else; caring for his sick family meant his business was dwindling.

One day a decrepit old man appeared. He introduced himself as Father Time. He said that if Mr Tempus would do his work for him, he would be given the gift of immortality and his son would be preserved and restored once the sentence had been carried out.

Wanting nothing but to save his son, Mr Tempus signed the contract given to him. His own youth slipped through his fingers, and a mysterious force began taking over his house. Suddenly, the tiny broom cupboard upstairs became a vast space where he would do the work Father Time gave to him. The back door quadrupled in size and became what Father Time described as a portal to the Otherworld, so he could drop in and make sure Mr Tempus was sticking to his side of the bargain.

Eventually Mr Tempus built up his business again, and tried to get used to being alone. Before long creatures from the Otherworld heard about the little shop and came to visit, as well the mortal customers that simply knew Mr Tempus as a lonesome old man who knew little of life outside of watches.

Mr Tempus opened his eyes to find his cheeks damp with tears, as a new prisoner was being ejected roughly into the cell. The unconscious prisoner fell to the floor with a dull thump.

Mr Tempus stood to see Sheridan opening his eyes briefly before closing them again.

"The only thing that can cure my headache is toast smothered with quince jam," Sheridan muttered.

Mr Tempus tried not to laugh at the dragon; even in the most hopeless situation he was still thinking about his stomach. He wasn't entirely sure if Sheridan was awake, or talking in his sleep.

"Do stop twisting my arm, now. My wings have gone numb. This house has too many drafts, Uncle."

"Sheridan," Mr Tempus whispered urgently.

"I'll be up in a minute, Uncle," Sheridan mumbled.

"Sheridan!" Mr Tempus tried again, shaking the dragon's shoulder.

Sheridan opened his eyes. He was wrapped in a thick and very cold net. He looked up and rubbed his throbbing head.

"Mr Tempus!" Sheridan exclaimed, as he realised he had finally found the little watchmaker.

"Shush!" said Mr Tempus harshly. "If they realise you've woken they might move you! What happened?"

"We were trying to find you! My uncle sent us to see the enchantress at Tempura-Sleus, but we were ambushed by a gang of nixies!"

"We?"

"Letisha and I," said the dragon. "Thankfully she escaped. Hopefully she is with Mrs Grisham's Ghost."

"Letisha is here?" Mr Tempus exclaimed. He shook his head, and then looked intently at the dragon. "I assume you've realised this is about the um…" he twiddled his thumbs and struggled to describe something. Sheridan shrugged, confused. Mr Tempus tapped the small pocket of his waistcoat where his watch would normally live, had it not been taken by the nixies.

"Ah, if you are talking about the 'um…'" Sheridan copied the gesture. "I believe it is with the witch, or possibly still with Letisha."

"Did you say Letisha?" called another voice from the next cell. A thin hand reached through, and a stern-faced woman appeared at the bars. "She's the cause of all this trouble."

"She's not, Liz," said Mr Tempus tiresomely. Their cells were only a few feet apart and still they had remained silent. "The only person to blame here is me."

"As soon as I can contact my solicitor, I am suing you, Mr Tempus," said Aunt Stackhouse. "But not before we begin to mention the trouble you will be in for endangering a child. It's simply not acceptable."

Mr Tempus ignored her completely. "Sheridan, do you think you could melt the bars?"

"I don't think so," said the dragon. "I used up my reserves melting the nixies that tried to take Letisha. Unless there is anything I could eat to stoke me up again, I'm afraid we're going nowhere. Look," he sighed, patting his pockets. "They've taken all my beautiful watches, even the one Letisha gave me!"

"You," Aunt Stackhouse interrupted his lament, "Have a ridiculous lisp. It should have been corrected."

Sheridan gasped. "Madam, when you are as old as I, you begin to worry less about little flaws and more about the fact that there is a child out there, lost and alone, with dangerous creatures after her for reasons she doesn't understand. You are the ridiculous one, not I."

Mr Tempus smiled smugly as Aunt Stackhouse was successfully silenced. Of all the people who would prove useless when stuck in the dungeons of the Fortress of Malice, she was definitely in his top ten.

"Did this enchantress say anything useful?" asked Mr Tempus.

"She took Letisha away after we were playing with the…you know… and then the next thing I knew the cavern was swarming with nixies and I had to fly through the ceiling! I caught up with Letisha and they pelted us with hailstones and we crashed. Letisha hid and they dragged me here.

Mind you, the way my head feels I think they kicked me most of the way! But I knew if they brought me here I could find you and help you escape…"

Sheridan silenced himself as tiny feet echoed on the floor. A gang of nixies leered through the icy bars at him. Under the damp net he failed to look very ferocious even as he bared his teeth. The nixies cackled and taunted, before a voice silenced them.

"So," it grumbled, "I send you to fetch me a mortal, and you bring a dragon. What if I had asked you to bring me a dragon?!"

Mr Tempus shrunk back. Sheridan ached too much to move.

The hooded man moved closer. "So, dragon, where is the girl? Did you eat her, perchance?"

"I would never!" Sheridan exclaimed.

"Of course not. You were too cowardly to even fight off my little nixies."

Sheridan folded his arms as best he could. "It was hardly a fair fight. Give me a good scuttle of kindling and I would melt this place to the ground, nixies and all."

The hooded man sniffed, and turned to Aunt Stackhouse.

"And you. You've lied to me, haven't you? I ought to take your tongue again just for that!"

"That would be most welcome!" Sheridan interjected.

"I've told you what you wanted to know!" cried Aunt Stackhouse. "I've got nothing more to give you."

"Oh, I don't know about that," he said, and turned to look at her as much as possible; the hood was still obscuring his face. "Your time might be useful, if nothing else. You've got to be only, what, forty, fifty at the most?"

"That's none of your business!" she snapped.

Jack placed his veined, pallid hand on the back of his hooded head. "I am running low on time, you see. A healthy mortal such as yourself should have at least forty years of time left. I could use forty years."

With that, he pulled down the black hood, and revealed his face to her. She screamed as Sheridan simply looked away. Only Mr Tempus could see an insipid scalp, flecked with straggling hair so thin and white it was barely visible, and a set of near transparent pointed ears. Vertebra almost stuck through his grossly skinny neck.

Aunt Stackhouse was reduced to a weeping wreck on the floor, as Jack pulled his hood about his face once more.

"Time makes fools of us all, especially if we are running out of it. So yes," Jack said, stroking a boney finger over her hair, "I could use forty years."

22

IN THE HALL OF THE ARCHITECTS

Letisha was beginning to regret dreaming Mrs Grisham's Ghost into the inn, as she continued to mock and ridicule everyone around her.

"And another thing," said the ghost, moving on to find something else to complain about, as she had finished criticising a sprite with a crooked hat. "I am certain that somebody is smuggling their own spirits into this tavern! I can smell it!"

"There is only one spirit in here," a familiar voice twinkled with wit.

Letisha turned to find that the Duke of Quill had come to her rescue for the second time.

The Duke began to sit down, almost on top of Mrs Grisham's Ghost, who moved quickly out of the way, screwing up her face in disgust.

"I'm so glad to see you, Duke," Letisha tried to hold back tears of relief at the sight of a friendly face. "Things have gone very wrong."

"Oh dear," he said. "I heard you talking to the barman and thought you might need some help."

"How did you know…?"

"About the spirit?" he opened his coat and revealed row upon row of tiny colourful glimmering bottles. "I have ways. Ghosts move in the same way as dreams, you know." The Duke produced an embossed business card from his sleeve and pushed it across the table. Letisha read it aloud.

"'Nelson, Duke of Quill, qualified Dreamseller, as certified by the League of Dreamsellers'."

"Oh!" She cried. "You're a Dreamseller too!"

"Why," he hushed his voice. "Are you a Dreamseller? I haven't seen you at any of the meetings, or your invisible friend over there. Just how did you come by your unusual mode of transport?" He pointed to the bottle poking out of Letisha's bag.

"Another Dreamseller gave it to me, actually. Mr Horatio Dreamseller. Perhaps you know him?"

The Duke produced a small leather book, after which he licked his finger and flipped through the pages.

"Nope, there is no Horatio Dreamseller in the Dreamsellers Directory. Are you lying to me?"

Letisha sighed and ran a hand over her face. "Mrs Grisham's Ghost, will you please tell this man that there is a Horatio Dreamseller and he comes to Mr Tempus's shop on a regular basis, and I was given this Waking Dream as a gift. I didn't know what it was or how to use it, and I only picked it for the colour. And if you're a Duke, why are you selling dreams, anyway?"

The Duke withdrew his card. "After all the great battles I had little else to do with my time, so I decided to travel and provide a service. When you're blind in one eye and missing a few too many bits no crusade will take you. I may be retired, but I do have hobbies, you know." The Duke paused. "I know a damsel in distress when I see one. Weren't you older the last time I saw you?"

"I'm not a damsel in distress," she snapped, but then sighed reproachfully, disappointed that he had noticed her transformation. "It's been a rough night. I lost Sheridan to the nixies, and I think they've taken him to Malice."

"I thought you'd need help from the moment I met you; I've always had a nose for sniffing out trouble. If you're heading to the Fortress of Malice…"

"We don't need your help," snapped Mrs Grisham's Ghost, "Anymore than I need a hat and scarf to keep the cold out."

"You're walking around with a mortal and using a phoney bottled dream to travel to one of the most dangerous places in this part of the Otherworld. Will you be able to protect her, spirit?"
The ghost hung her head.

"I can't afford a bodyguard," Letisha said, standing with the clock in her hand. She had had enough of his tall tales. She was unnerved that the Dreamseller whose potion she was using was bogus. Her only goal was to reach Sheridan and Mr Tempus. Now she was dry and had an idea of where she was going, she tried to prepare herself. The clock and the ghost might not be much company, but at least she was not alone.

*

A table laid with a hundred delicious dishes sat in an atmosphere so frosty it was a miracle the wine didn't freeze. In the centre of the spread was an impressive stuffed peacock, its beady eyes fixed in a tragic glassy stare. Candles lined each wall, still tall as if they were newly lit, even though they had been burning for centuries. At one end of the table, Mother Earth sat in her glimmering finery, a veil hiding her face as she looked disdainfully at the banquet, most of which she knew would go to waste.
At the other end Father Time contemplated his wine, swishing it thoughtfully round a tall thin glass. He kept to the shadows, as the darkened wall and part

of the ceiling behind him undulated with tickers, clanking and moving over another as they waited for scraps from the table.

Jack Frost sat in the middle of the table. He shovelled food into his disgusting little mouth as fast as he could manage, tearing spitefully at the meat and throwing what he didn't fancy to the floor. A line of tickers enthusiastically made their way over to indulge what he left. He still kept his ruined face covered, as if he feared he might fall apart at any moment. His grubby hands snatched at every plate within his reach, grabbing for more wine jelly, seeded bread, sticky pork, rare truffles and quail eggs boiled in their shells.

Mother Earth grimaced;

"You greedy little grub; you never eat unless it's provided by somebody else. Are you even going to eat that peacock?"

"His nixies will enjoy it. Its meat will feed their village for a week," Father Time responded simply, sipping his wine. His voice was gentle, even when asking for trouble. "Is something troubling you, Mother?"

Mother Earth closed her eyes, breathed out and laid her hands in her lap.

"You know very well what is troubling me, Father; I hate these 'compulsory' dinners in which we pretend that everything is normal and we don't hate each other."

"I wish you'd talk civilly," Father Time spat.

"I wish you'd behave civilly," she fired back.

He raised his eyebrows. "It's not like I threw the world out of balance by abandoning my duties."

"You drove me away," she said calmly. "I am not a possession to be owned."

"You're a woman, aren't you?"

Jack Frost chuckled, before demanding a group of cowering nixies waiting on the enormous table bring him more wine. They scattered in all directions as he hurled a plate of prawns at them, showering the floor with shellfish and dressing.

"You," said Jack Frost.

A terrified Nixie pointed shakily to herself.

He nodded. "Come here."

The Nixie shook the prawns off her tatty dress and approached the table. She glanced hopefully at Mother Earth, silently begging for help. Mother Earth was reluctant to interfere, desperately trying to conserve her power.

"You have displeased me tonight," said Jack Frost, placing a cold finger under the nixie's chin. "It's only a shame the others got away."

With that the Nixie froze, her pale eyes widening until she was simply a solid figure of ice. Jack pressed his finger against her flat little nose and pushed her over. Her body shattered against the marble floor.

"If you would let me be, I could fix things," Mother Earth said, tears pouring down her cheeks.

"Now why would I do that when it would mean I lose my beloved wife? You're interfering and not letting the scenario run its natural course. Just hand the Ouroboros over to Jack and we can end this perpetual winter once and for all."

"If he wanted to trade off his most prized possession for things beyond his inferior little grasp then that's his fault," she snapped, and sipped her wine to prevent herself from spitting more venom. She knew that it was her job to be cruel, but when it was unnecessary she tried to refrain.

"You've involved a mortal in the business of the Architects, Mother. There are consequences for your actions." Father Time mused with an evil grin.

"You speak in silly riddles. Letisha Tate is a good girl and I won't have her harmed. As for Mr Tempus…"

"We all know how you feel about Mr Tempus," Frost said mockingly.

"If you would have taken the hint and come back to me, there would be no problems," Father Time paused, "and I could have released him."

"He has served his sentence," Mother Earth tried to keep her tone cool. She could be sweet when she wanted to, but being kind to him sickened her. "If you release Tempus and his son, then perhaps we can be friends."

"If you give back the Ouroboros, I will release Tempus."

"If you release Tempus, I will give back the Ouroboros," Mother Earth replied. Her eyes glowed, and flickered from the colours of spring to autumn. "I know that the both of you have grown bitter over the years, because of me in one way or another. When will you learn that you cannot possess another person anymore than you can possess Time itself? Resentment has clouded your judgement."
Father Time tried to speak, but she cut him off.

"And as for interfering by giving a mortal a bottled dream, anyone would think you were inviting a challenge."

"You've been helping too," Jack Frost grumbled with his mouth full once more. Compared to his fellow Architects he behaved like a spoiled child at these compulsory banquets, despite lording over the nixies with an iron fist. He loved nothing more than to plant the seeds of disagreement and then sit back and watch an argument blossom between his peers. He pointed a half-eaten turkey leg at Father Time. "Time told me about it; helping her when she shouldn't even be here? Naughty, naughty."

Mother Earth narrowed her eyes. "I happen to like Letisha. Her heart is in the right place. And she picked Waking Dream, Father. She could have chosen Forever Falling, or Recurring Embarrassment. What else have you been selling under your false name? Has the League found out you're impersonating one of their brethren yet?"

"I'll have you know I'm a fantastic Dreamseller. Everyone needs a hobby," Father Time folded his arms and tucked his hands into his long sleeves. "The League of Dreamsellers are a crafty bunch of scoundrels who would not sit idly by if I was misrepresenting them." Time did not completely believe his own hype, unsure how the League would react if they discovered their products were being imitated. His disguise would soon be revealed and he would have to find another name to travel under.

Mother Earth scowled at his excuses. She did not approve of how he paraded himself about under such an eccentric guise. The work of an architect meant one had to be all seeing, compassionate, and level headed, but it was lonely work since the three had become so bitter and distant. While they chose to take solid and
 more human forms for their own varying reasons, they were only entities at the end of it, spirits that were created to serve and protect the very elements of the universe.

Mother Earth knew that secretly Father Time despised Jack Frost, whom they both saw as stupid, greedy and destructive. He left a trail of devastation wherever he went, the effects permanent if not appropriately dealt with. Malice had once been a lush and vibrant kingdom simply with an unfortunate name, but it was now dead and barren. Father Time knew that Frost had attempted to steal Mother Earth away, and was still working towards that goal, even as she shunned him.

Time pressed his fingers together, contemplating a scheme. "I know you like a challenge."

Mother Earth narrowed her eyes. "And I know you won't just let Letisha walk into Malice."

"I certainly will not!" yowled Jack Frost. "Time, you rally the tickers, and I'll rally the nixies! I've come too far to let everything slip now!"

"Be quiet," snapped Father Time. "I have a proposal for you, since you have so much faith in one little mortal. My contract with Tempus is almost up, and frankly I've become quite fond of having all this free time and the power of the Ouroboros. If Letisha Tate can reach Tempus within six hours, I will let him walk out of Malice and back into the mortal world."

"What about the boy?" asked Mother Earth.

"Insurance," said Father Time simply.

In an instant she sat not at the opposite end of the table, but beside him, her face an inch from his, and her eyes burning fearsome gold.

"That's not fair," she said.

"Neither is leaving your rightful husband for a mortal man," Father Time said flatly. "You dug your grave, now lie in it." His voice echoed around the dark grey stone walls and grand gothic columns of the great chamber.

Jack Frost chewed slowly so as not to miss anything.

"Would you really deprive a man of his only son after he has served you for all these years just to win him back?" begged Mother Earth softly. "Does the love a father has for his son mean so little to you?"

"I have set the challenge. If Letisha can get him out in less than six hours, I will let him go. Anything else you choose to do is up to you, or indeed to this foolish child you're putting so much stock in. Don't expect me to just lie back and let you win." He leaned forward, his eyes darkening and his face clouding. His voice deepened slightly, and he showed his true age despite a youthful visage. "You hurt me beyond repair."

Mother Earth folded her arms and leaned back in her chair once more.

"I accept the challenge," she said, feeling a faint sense of confidence. "Let the fate of Peter Tempus lie with Letisha Tate."

23

BREAKING THE FORTRESS

Letisha was beginning to question her sanity as she stood outside The Maiden's Arms with Mrs Grisham's Ghost and the Duke beside her. They were preparing to leave Gram Shank.

"Now," said the Duke. "You've used Waking Dream before so I won't patronise you as to what to do, only…"

"Only what, you great fool?" snapped Mrs Grisham's Ghost.

"You've never actually been to Malice, have you?"

Letisha shook her head.

"What I suggest is I take the lead and dream you there; I've been before, in the great battle of Rig Snug, many years ago…"

"Just shut up and do it," bit the ghost. "And see you don't leave me at this filthy tavern."

The Duke ignored her and sipped from a bottle taken from his coat. Within seconds the air around him puckered and rippled, until he simply popped out of the night as if he had been plucked from reality altogether. Letisha gasped as the falling snow began to fill his footprints.

"He doesn't know what he's talking abo…" Mrs Grisham's Ghost trailed off as Letisha vanished too, and left her alone. "Don't you dare leave me here!" she screeched. "This is absolute lunacy!"

Letisha felt as if her stomach was rumbling so powerfully it rippled up and down her body and along her arms and legs. Colours flashed before her eyes, blue turned to purple, then to red and then to black. A blast of freezing wind very nearly blew her out of her oversized boots.

They stood on the edge of a crossroads, the cobbles barely visible through the blizzard. Letisha could feel the hard ancient road beneath her, but she could not see anything more than three feet away. The darkness was absolute, a crushing void much like the one she had fallen into off the edge of the porch. Letisha was actually relieved as Mrs Grisham's Ghost began to materialise, giving off a faint eerie glow.

Inside Letisha's satchel, the little clock clattered and quaked. She placed her hand inside to comfort it.

The Duke scratched his bristled chin and looked around like a commodore surveying an ocean, even though there was little to see beyond the ghost's iridescence.

"So where's the fortress?" Letisha shouted over the wind. The squinting Duke didn't fill her with confidence.

"I might have made a mistake," he admitted. He lit a tiny lantern he pulled from inside his coat. A small flame struggled against the wind as he took out an old map. "Ah!" he exclaimed, blowing snowflakes off the ragged paper.

"What?" Letisha pulled her collar up. As her eyes adjusted she realised they were very high up. Lights were visible in the distance. Though the houses were too far away to see clearly, she was able to determine a hillside. Snow blanketed the landscape, covering anything by which they might pinpoint their location. The snowflakes were bigger than marbles and falling faster and faster. She was thankful that her boots were waterproof, as she could feel her hair and clothes becoming damp once more. The snow was snuffing the ghost's glow, though she did not flinch from the cold. Normally the idea of snow filled Letisha with glee, where her parents complained about roads and public transport grinding to a painful halt. Only now did she agree with them, since she had no idea how the weather might affect their journey.

"We're only a little way off," the Duke grunted at last, relief in his voice. "I believe we are near Hung Cross."

"Where?!"

"The meeting point of the River Airvia, the great Blue River, and the smaller River Rig-Pug. Thank goodness we didn't land in the water!" Letisha's jaw dropped; she sincerely hoped he was joking

"See over there," the Duke pointed south. His freezing and unprotected fingers were rapidly turning blue. "That's the town of Pug." A tiny cluster of white lights was just about visible, flickering against the thickening gusts. The squat little black and white houses looked as though they were huddling together for warmth amidst the blizzard. Smoke plumed from their chimneys and almost froze in the sky. As the moonlight fought its way through the clouds, it was quite a pretty sight, like a Christmas card. The festive image didn't warm her for long, and Letisha longed for gloves more than anything. She was thankful her long hair kept her neck and ears so warm. They were not in a completely desolate landscape, as through the blizzard she noticed what looked to her like a chairlift, but was actually the rusting, partly demolished shaft of a mine. It rose up at a steep angle against the clouds like a shard of glass escaping the earth. She decided that there probably weren't many skiing tourists to provide a chairlift for.

"The mines are disused now," explained the Duke. "This is what is left behind. Once they hollowed everything useful out of the hillside they began building the fortress of Malice with the stones they pulled out of the earth. It's a huge structure, but it's easy to miss in this foul weather,"

"We're lost?" Letisha cried. "I trusted you!"

"Didn't I say it was lunacy?" said the ghost. The little clock jingled its agreement.

"No, no," said the Duke. "If Pug is south, then Malice is north."

They turned and saw that a great stone structure loomed ahead of them, barely visible through the thickening snowdrift. It had been cut into the mountains by many small, tried hands some centuries earlier. A few straggling cables linked the mineshaft to the fortress, but most were broken and buried in the snow, rusted and useless. Unlike Tempura-Sleus, it did not brim with natural beauty, nor did it
gleam with industry and production like Gram-Shank. It simply sat there menacingly, like a cat waiting to pounce. The mountain rose up either side of the fortress, blanketed in snow. Eerie blue torches burned here and there, barely making a pinprick in the darkness. The size of the structure was crushing. Even from a distance and with her view obscured, Letisha could tell that the walls were heavily armoured and ready for an assault from something far more threatening than a small girl, an ageing duke and a miserable spirit.

"We'll need a miracle to get in," Letisha muttered to the ghost.
The Duke continued to puzzle over his map, trying to decide where they had gone wrong.

"I'm no good at climbing. What about you?"

"It's too bad you found a half-wit in that tavern." Mrs Grisham's Ghost added. "You really do attract unpleasant types, don't you?"

Letisha folded her arms. "Like you?"
The ghost was quiet. As Letisha stroked the clock inside her bag, her hand clinked against something else; the bottle of Waking Dream found its way into her hand as though it were making a suggestion to be used.

"I have an idea," she said, taking a sip of the dream. "I'm not going to dream of Malice; I'm going to dream about Mr Tempus and Sheridan."

Sheridan was sitting up in his cell, nursing his tail. It had become bent in the attack, and now flopped at an awkward angle. His bones were stronger than steel so Mr Tempus knew he wasn't feeling any physical pain, but more the sorry acceptance that his tail would never be perfect again.

"It's not so bad," soothed Mr Tempus. "Who looks at only the tail of such an impressive dragon, anyway?"
Sheridan looked up and smiled slightly.

"Oh, it's not just that. Poor Letisha is lost in the Blue Mountains, lost and freezing, and it's all my fault! If I hadn't eaten so much at lunch I would have been faster!"

"Don't blame yourself," said Mr Tempus, and decided to change the subject. "Do you feel a spark yet?"
Sheridan cleared his throat and coughed. Normally he would be able to conjure a flame with little effort, but right now even melting ice was a challenge. He placed a hand to his brow dramatically.

"Alas! I am a dragon without a torch!"
As he said this, the air outside the cell holding Mr Tempus began to bubble and pucker, before two little striped legs appeared, under an oversized skirt and coat and finally a mass of messy hair. Letisha Tate stood in one piece, accompanied by a one-eyed man in uniform, and a disgruntled blue haze that could only be Mrs Grisham's Ghost.
Sheridan limped enthusiastically to the bars of his cell and hugged them, as he wanted to hug Letisha.

"Oh my clever little friend! How did you find us? And what happened to you? You're still so small!"

"The enchantress couldn't fix everything, but I had a little help from some friends," she said. "We need to get you out of here. Now."

Somewhere not too far away, Father Time sat pondering. He grew tired of his stay at Malice. Since giving up his tasks to Mr Tempus he did not have a set domain, so mostly he drifted from place to place as it suited him. Naturally when he convinced Frost that Tempus had his long lost Ouroboros, it made sense to hold the little watchmaker at Malice where escape would be impossible with the nixies on guard.
Time did not like the nixes. He had built his own minions, the tickers, from scratch. They were a delightful mix between insect and machine, and far superior to a hoard of scrabbling miners. Mother Earth settled for her vines,

which were fast in comparison to nixes, but didn't pack the same punch as a swarm of Tickers.

He went over in his head how he would punish the useless nixies before his time at Malice was through. The Tickers covering the wall behind him hummed gently, as if sharing his thoughts and malicious ideas. Their metallic wings flickered in irritation, as a single nixie poked her head round the great door at the far end of the room. She mustered her most attractive form so as not to displease him, knocking shyly with her white knuckles.

"My Lord?"

Time held up a hand to silence her as a single ticker buzzed beside his ear, uttering a message in its high, metallic voice.

"What is it, minion?" he mouthed irritably, trying to listen.

"About the arrangement with your wife…"

Time's eyes grew wide as the ticker finished speaking. Though he knew the nixie was about to tell him the same message, he allowed her to continue.

"What about it?"

"Well my Lord, if our calculations are correct, the mortal still has three hours left to help the watchmaker and the dragon escape…."

"And?"

"Well…" she was almost too terrified to speak.

"Spit it out, you stupid creature," snapped Father Time. The swarm of tickers behind him grew steadily louder.

"Well, my Lord, they seem to be escaping…right now."

Father Time tore the ticker from his shoulder with one hand and hurled his glass at the door with the other. The poor Nixie was showered with wine.

"Impossible! That child is never on time for anything!"

*

"We need to break the bars," said Mr Tempus. "There are no keys, only ice. Sheridan's too tired to do much of anything."

"I just need a spark!" cried the dragon.

"I can provide that, old boy," said the Duke as he produced a small and much loved silver lighter, which he held in front of Sheridan's open mouth. There was a snapping sound and a huge blue fireball left the dragon's jaws and shot clean through the icy bars, leaving a dripping hole just big enough for him to squeeze through. The fireball hurled across the passage, blackening the far wall and narrowly missing Letisha.

She helped Mr Tempus through the hole, before she noticed her aunt glaring out at her from the next cell.

"Now," she said, overly confident. "I know that can't possibly be Aunt Stackhouse."

"Letisha Tate, when I get out of here you'll be grounded for the rest of your natural life."

Letisha gulped as she realised that the impossible had occurred. She then remembered that there were a set of thick icy bars between them.

"That doesn't give me too much incentive to let you out does it?"

"And she made fun of my speech impediment!" Sheridan added. Letisha folded her arms.

"Being grounded is the last thing on my mind, Aunt Liz. Sheridan, if you wouldn't mind."

Sheridan sighed, took a deep breath, and was about to release her when the great black doors at the end of the dungeon were flung open. A swarm of nixies burst through with raging glee. They screeched, wielding weapons made of ice and hurling hailstones.

Without a second thought, Sheridan produced another flame and melted the first few rows of attackers, only to find the puddles reformed into fewer yet bigger creatures. Any tickers caught in the fire glowed white-hot.

"Quickly," said the Duke, drawing his sword. "I'll hold them off and you can get out!"

"What about you?" Letisha cried. "You can't possibly fight them all!"

"Just go! Sheridan, tell her!"

Sheridan shrugged as if to say the Duke knew what he was doing, as he blocked the blow of a fair sized hailstone.

"Through the doors behind them; that's our only way!" cried Mr Tempus as Letisha fumbled with her bottled dream. Clumsily, she removed the cork only to drop the bottle. It did not shatter, but she did manage to spill all but a drop.

"Save it!" said the Duke, swigging his own as he fought off the nixies with his other hand, or at least those that Sheridan wasn't melting.

In a flash Letisha, Mr Tempus and Sheridan were standing on the hillside on the other side of the fortress.

"Why did he do that?" Letisha cried tearfully, thankful she had managed to snatch her remaining dream, "They'll overpower him for sure!"

"He's a fool, and he's brave," said Mr Tempus.

"Poor Duke," Letisha shivered. "And what about my aunt?"

"Their quarrel isn't with Liz, she'll be fine. At worse, they'll come after us." Mr Tempus brightened slightly "I knew changing your clock would come in useful."

"What do you mean?" Letisha responded as they took to the air.

"Had I not done, the nixies would have been on us a lot quicker than they were."

24

THE FOURTH OUROBOROS

The Duke of Quill worried he had met his match as nixies toyed with him, attacking one or two at a time. Despite his best efforts, they were particularly difficult to exterminate as they did not fall like a normal beast, but shattered like ice. They then reformed into another creature. They hissed, spat and scratched with sharp fingers, but the Duke fought valiantly. He was determined to buy enough time for his friends to escape. nixies were stupid and easily distracted, and though he felt his limbs tiring he knew he could win. He felt inside his coat for any potion he might have that might help, but struggled with his damaged hand, and received a large hailstone to the head that made his vision blur. He heard a different set of footsteps on the icy floor, and another, as the nixies parted and two men entered.

The Duke knew very little of the folklore Letisha had learned so much of during her unscheduled visit to the Otherworld, but he knew he was looking at Father Time and a somewhat dishevelled Jack Frost. Neither of them held a weapon. Father Time conjured a small, very battered looking pocket watch in his gloved hand and very solemnly said,
        "Nelson, Duke of Quill, I do believe your time is up."
With a long finger, he flipped open the watch and simply stopped the cogs. The duke froze in mid attack, his mouth snarling with the thrill of the battle and the shock of being paused so abruptly. He became very grey, just before a green vapour left his nose and mouth and made its way towards Jack Frost. Frost took a deep breath, inhaling the time. In a second, there was nothing but a pile of ashes on the cold floor where the Duke had stood. The nixies cheered gleefully, though looked slightly disappointed for not being able to take down the intruder for themselves.
Jack Frost stood a little taller and his skin was less translucent, but he was no less frosty looking. He had plumped out and regained most of his fine white hair.
As she hovered invisibly in the cell beside the cowering Aunt Stackhouse, who had sadly been left behind, Mrs Grisham's Ghost saw something in Jack Frost that reminded her of somebody she once knew, a long time ago. Bitterness and revelation turned her heart sour.

*

"So where do we go now?" Letisha shouted over the wind. They had been standing in the snow for only a moment and already she was freezing.

"What's that?" Mr Tempus cut in, pointing. A single blue light danced through the blizzard and swayed hypnotically in front of them. They all jumped as it spoke.

"Letisha," the orb said. "You are all in danger. It is only a matter of time until Jack Frost is strong enough to retrieve his Ouroboros, and then all is lost. Unless you can help."

"What can I do?" Letisha asked. She barely recognised Selena's voice as she spoke through the orb.

"You must retrieve the Fourth Ouroboros, a machine of purity that does not carry the bitterness of its owner. It is an instrument beyond the Architects, built by mortal hands."

Letisha didn't see Mr Tempus shuffling awkwardly, but Sheridan did.

"Mr Tempus, we thought that there were only three. What's she talking about?"

"It's nothing," he said, wringing his hands and shivering. "I was tinkering about in the workshop years ago. After I looked at the book I gave to you, Letisha, I … I might have managed to build a working Ouroboros. I gave the original to Sheridan because I knew he would take care of it, and I kept the one I had built a secret. But it went missing."

"Not so," said the Orb. "It is in a safe place. You must find it."

"But where is it?" Letisha asked. "And how?"

"The Waking Dream."

"But how do you know all this?" Mr Tempus asked the Orb. "Who are you?"

"A friend," said the Orb. "You have to trust me for the sake of your son. Find the Fourth Ouroboros before all is lost!"

The orb faded from bright blue to white, before vanishing, allowing darkness to prevail.

Mr Tempus groaned in distress.
"Oh, my dear Letisha, you are such a good girl. I am so sorry for dragging you into all this. And Sheridan, I only gave you that Ouroboros because I thought it would go in your collection and be kept under lock and key for the foreseeable future."

"Why did you build another one?" said Letisha.

"Because I could," he shrugged. "I've been pretty lonely these past decades, you know."

"Is that the only reason?" Sheridan folded his arms sternly.

"Well," said the little watchmaker, "I never really took the time to learn to use the Ouroboros, but you never know when you might need these things."

Sheridan and Letisha looked at each other in confusion, and then back at Mr Tempus.

"When I made my deal with Father Time and he took my son away, I noticed the watch he carried with him." Mr Tempus explained. "I knew he was a proud creature so I asked him about it. He told me very little so I gathered some research from the various companies I did work for. It's amazing how many people have written about the Ouroboros over the years, though of course it's all just dismissed as myth.

"Finally I realised that the very item I coveted was in fact detailed in a book given to me by my dear departed wife; your book. I managed to cobble together a working Ouroboros. It didn't look like the others because I made it from scrap and reclaimed silver, but it did the job. I had time aplenty to fill the vial to make it work. I never used it, of course. I thought if I did it might upset the balance, but I see that has been done anyway.

"I came across a real Ouroboros purely by accident. I was in London on business when I spotted it in an antique shop. I bought it for next to nothing. Then I presented it to you, Sheridan. How long ago was that?"

"It's got to be at least eighty years," Sheridan admitted with a slightly baffled expression. "I'd forgotten all about it until I saw the picture in the book. Uncle simply told me to give it to Selena, he didn't know there was a fourth one at all."

Mr Tempus frowned, confused. "Who is Selena, anyway?"

"The enchantress," said Letisha. "I found her poking about in the stockroom on my first morning, and she convinced me she was a dream." Sheridan frowned, remembering how Letisha had already mentioned meeting Selena.

"Why didn't you tell me you'd met before?"

"I made a promise…" Letisha looked at him guiltily. She would never get used to being so small, she decided. "I said I wouldn't tell anyone we'd met, but I thought she was just a silly dream and it didn't matter. Then Uncle Sigmund sent us to see her, but she didn't help us at all. She got Sheridan kidnapped and left me freezing in the middle of nowhere. And I'm still only seven years old! It was only because of Mrs Grisham's Ghost… where do you think she might have got to?"

"'Still inside, I should imagine," said Mr Tempus. "She can look after herself, but there's still the matter of my son. Now you have broken me out, I don't know if he will be released so easily. You see, it wasn't so simple as doing a few odd tasks for Father Time. When I took his job, I also took his form; I was still a youngster, and he was a withered old man. I don't doubt he has grown to like being young again."

Letisha was confused and frustrated. She crouched down in the snow and took the book out of her satchel, followed by the bottle of Waking Dream. It had only a single drop of viscous violet liquid shimmering at its base. The clock trundled out too, stretched its bells and then wagged its behind when it saw Mr Tempus.

"Ah, my little lovely!" he said, bending to retrieve it.

"It followed me," Letisha explained. "Before I came through the portal with Sheridan, I found it in the Watch Room. It was all dirty and covered in cobwebs, as though it hadn't been touched for a hundred years."

"Look at that," Mr Tempus pointed to the face of the clock, where another even had appeared underneath her date of birth. "'Letisha enters the Otherworld'."

"What does it mean?"

"It means that your coming here will have a profound influence on the rest of your life. Clearly you were meant to follow me through, just as I was probably meant to be taken," said Mr Tempus, and went on to reminisce about his work as the Great Timekeeper. As he did this, Letisha opened the book to the page of the Ouroboros. She searched the diagrams for a clue. Being a little older, her reading had improved and it made more sense. At that moment she truly loathed the enchantress for making everything so secretive and complicated. Why couldn't people just spell things out?

As she looked at the page, the diagram of the green liquid shimmered slightly; surely her eyes were playing tricks on her. She blinked forcefully in disbelief, only to see it again.

Letisha uncorked the bottle of Waking Dream and just about managed to coax the last drop onto her tongue. She had no intention of travelling, so instead she concentrated on the glimmering page until the paper rippled like muddy water. She poked the page, surprised to find it had the resistant texture of porridge, liquid enough to push her hands in. Steeling herself, she reached in as deep as her elbows. The liquid paper was like nothing she'd ever experienced, warm and thick, smelling of libraries, and a relief from the bitter weather.

Sheridan happened to turn and see what she was doing. He bit the claws on one hand and pointed in silence with the other, as Letisha managed to grasp hold of something. It was like pulling a spoon out of treacle. Whatever it was didn't want to come without a fight. Her arms had been pulled deeper into the page, so much so that she was lying on her chest, shoulder deep and dipping her chin in the paper porridge. It pulled like quicksand, and it was only because of Sheridan and Mr Tempus hauling her back that she didn't disappear inside the book altogether.

With her hands wrapped around a smooth round object, Letisha finally came loose. She flew backwards into the dragon and the watchmaker. Freed from the book, they laughed as they all collected themselves from the ground. Letisha stood, dusted herself off and opened her hands.

Within her grasp was a very ordinary looking pocket watch, with a plain silver case. She clicked it open past its numbered face to reveal a second face and a little green vial that bubbled and churned as though it were happy to see her.

"That's it," Mr Tempus whispered. "The Ouroboros I built, all those years ago."

She handed it to him and he cradled it like a baby bird. He had tears in his eyes, as though remembering something beautiful and painful all at the same time.

"Mr Tempus?" Letisha said. "Are you alright?"

"I remember her," he said simply. "I remember Anna."

He closed the Ouroboros to the numbered face, and showed them a photograph that had been fixed to the inside of the case. It was clearly very old, but in immaculate condition. It showed a woman with vibrant eyes and a pretty face, soft and caring. Both Letisha and Sheridan recognised her immediately.

"Is that...?" Sheridan began.

"My wife," said Mr Tempus. "Anna; Toby's mother. It's the only picture I ever had of her. I thought it was lost."

"But that's Selena," said Letisha.

"What?"

"I mean the hair's a bit different, but that's definitely her."

"You mean...she's alive?"

"She is a very powerful enchantress, Mr Tempus," added Sheridan.

"Well, where is she?" said Mr Tempus, steeled and determined. "I must see her."

25

MR GRISHAM REVEALED

Jack Frost paced the cavern, briefly stopping to drag his foot across the dusty patch left by the recently deceased Duke of Quill. Aunt Stackhouse watched him disdainfully as he moved, half limping with age and decay even after regaining some of his strength. She didn't stare long before he turned and shot her a look. His eyes glowed like embers, sunk into the grey surface of his face.

"You look at me like my wife used to, you know," he said.

Aunt Stackhouse muttered something.

"What was that, my one and only much appreciated remaining prisoner?"

Aunt Stackhouse coated her words with honey, fearing his wrath. "I said; you don't seem like the marrying type."

"Well, it didn't suit me, since I never married the right woman. But I'm sure she felt the same way in the end. I still think fondly of her from time to time."

Aunt Stackhouse glared, knowing as she looked into his eyes that he had taken that ridiculous Duke's time, just as he said he would take hers. The Duke was ancient, and probably had little left anyway, but she saw his vitality dancing behind Jack's eyes, a menacing reminder of her own potential demise.

"Her name was Una," he said. "Meaning 'the first'. I suppose it was apt really. She was a highborn, used to the finer things and horribly spoiled. Her temper was something similar to mine. It was her fire that attracted me. You know, opposites?"

Aunt Stackhouse frowned and shook her head.

"Fire and Ice, of course. But she didn't melt my heart for long, if at all I have one. I must have, somewhere, as even when I lived with Una I had feelings for another altogether more spectacular woman. She was married of course, and even though we were friends she had no idea of how I loved her. It's always the way isn't it? Have you ever experienced unrequited love?"

Aunt Stackhouse shook her head, lying.

"It almost destroyed me," he shook his head. "I am only a shadow of what I once was. The lord of the weather, of the rain and snow, is hardly expected to be shambling about in rags as you see me. But I gave everything

I had to try to win this woman, as I saw her own marriage crumbling. When I thought I had a chance to be happy, I left Una.

"I knew that she would try to pursue me across the moors on which our mansion sat, even though I was long gone, so I decided to put her to one final use. I sent the hardest frost the country had ever seen…"

Aunt Stackhouse's eyes welled. "How could you?"

"She was stupid enough to follow me out onto the moors in a blizzard to end all blizzards in little more than her nightgown. Is it any wonder she succumbed to exposure so quickly? Fifty-five wasn't a terribly young age to go. She bored me to tears anyway. She was buried in a fancy grave after they found her, frozen solid. I doubt anyone even attended the funeral; everyone hated her. They only came to the parties because of me.

"I took what little she had to aid my journey, but it didn't last long. So I traded the last thing of value I owned; the very implement that made taking time so easy. It's not good to do it with bare hands, you know." He yawned; some of his teeth were growing back. "Finishing off that sword waving fool has done me in for the night, and I didn't even do that alone.

"But don't worry," he tapped Aunt Stackhouse on the nose. "When I have my Ouroboros back, taking your time will be quite easy. I daresay I will enjoy it."

Aunt Stackhouse sat back in her cell and rubbed her arms for warmth. Jack brought cold and decay wherever he went. As she watched her breath dance away from her, the light grew slightly brighter. An eerie blue glow began to turn to raging red.

Aunt Stackhouse shrieked, as a spectral woman appeared beside her in a bedraggled nightgown. Her white hair flailed and her pale eyes glowered.

"Hell hath no fury like a woman scorned!" the apparition screeched. "I knew I recognised that scoundrel!"

Aunt Stackhouse was struck dumb.

"They always called him Frosty Jack when we were married. The 'popular one', he says! He never had any friends!"

Aunt Stackhouse attempted to get a word in. "W – who are you?"

"I," said the ghost, "Am the ghost of Mrs Una Grisham. And that rat calling himself Jack Frost is nothing more than Frosty Jack Grisham; the murdering villain I once married."

Father Time was restless. With all the control of Time at his fingertips, falling asleep and waking up exactly when he wanted was as easy as snapping his fingers, but on this particular morning, he found no rest. Around him a great mass of clocks all ticked to their own beat and schedule. Time paced up and down, his feet beating off the ground to the rhythm of a particularly large grandfather clock in the corner. He stopped at the far end of the room, his face level with that of a boy of twelve, with dark tousled hair and long eyelashes. He was held in an enormous bell jar, suspended in the green liquid that Father Time controlled so freely.

Father Time regarded the boy.

"It seems that I might be hanging onto you for a little longer than first planned, Master Tempus."

The boy did not reply. Even in his unconscious state, Time felt no sympathy for him; he was insurance and nothing else.

Father Time took his Ouroboros from his robes and flipped it open to the third face. The pawn cog showed that he still had control over Jack Frost, since his fellow architect was so weak. For a long time, Frost had relied on him for just about everything since he had all but sold his very essence in order to win Mother Earth. Now, as he became stronger, it would be harder to conceal that he had been nothing but a pawn in Times ultimate plan to punish Mr Tempus. Time had given up his Watch Room so needed a place to work from, but he still had his beloved Tickers. Soon, he knew he would have to surrender Frosts' power, his freedom, and the nixies.

Keeping Toby Tempus suspended took a good chunk of power, but it was not nearly so annoying as his inability to control Letisha Tate. He knew that Mr Tempus had altered her clock so that she was running minutes ahead of her natural time, but something else was protecting her, and he had a very good idea of who was to blame.

Having put all his own duties onto the mortal Peter Tempus meant he could have little control over him, but the fear he instilled was enough to keep him in line. Tempus didn't have the guts to do anything stupid.

He tapped the little vial of his Ouroboros impatiently. He had good instincts, but he was not a good judge of character. He had always thought that his wife was a selfish, spiteful character, but he would never describe his own behaviour as such. Mother Earth, with whom he had spent most of his career as Father Time, had managed to keep her mortal life with Peter Tempus a secret while working as an Architect.

Mr Tempus had no idea that Time had suspended his son in a vat of concentrated Time, keeping him close to ensure nobody would interfere. It was hard work collecting time and keeping it in such quantities, but he was strong and powerful.

Meanwhile, while she had had her mortal body destroyed, Mother Earth would have to watch, helpless to intervene unless she wanted to see her son come to harm. Father Time had threatened her on several occasions.

It was all so deliciously evil, he thought, as he rubbed his hands together.

"Time makes fools of everyone," he said aloud to the boy in the jar. As usual Toby did not respond, his hair and clothes moving slowly with the gelatinous liquid. "But nobody makes a fool out of Time."

26

BACK TO THE WATCH ROOM

"There is no way of getting back into Malice other than by flight," said Mr Tempus. "Sheridan, do you think you could manage?"

"We don't need to get into Malice," Letisha interrupted

"What do you mean?" Mr Tempus looked at her as though she had finally snapped.

"Biscuit wrappers," she grinned cunningly, unable to resist having just a little fun with him. Finally, it all made sense; the layers of existence stacked on top of one another like the clear plastic on top of the newspaper were Time's cruel trick.

"I remember what my Dad always says when I'm late; 'Time makes fools out of us all'. Surely if Time is a real person there's got to be something behind that. If he wanted to make a fool of you, he'd keep your son somewhere obvious," Letisha finished, taking her time so as not to get lost.

"But what has all this got to do with biscuits?" Sheridan said, scratching his horned head. "I'd love a biscuit, if you've got one."

"Keeping Toby in a guarded fortress is pointless when Time could keep him somewhere right under your nose."

Mr Tempus's brow crinkled. "Why do you think that?"

"It's like you explained to me, with the newspaper and the biscuit wrapper. Your shop is the newspaper; a world we can all see. The Watch Room is the biscuit wrapper you put on top, that you can only see when you know how. Couldn't Father Time simply put another layer on top of that and keep Toby there?"

Suddenly it all made sense to Letisha; it explained perfectly why the initials had appeared on her mirror. T.T. was Toby Tempus. She and Toby were in the same place, only on different layers.

Mr Tempus scratched his chin only momentarily, before saying, "You think Toby is in the Watch Room?"

Letisha hoped she was making sense. "It suddenly occurred to me that the Watch Room is somewhere that appears to exist in both worlds; I saw it in your shop, and then Selena showed me too. Also, whenever I'm in the room Toby used to sleep in I get the feeling I'm not alone, as if he's still there. You, your son and Father Time have always been in the same place."

"He'll never really escape from his duties," Mr Tempus spoke quietly, his eyes glowing as though a light bulb had been switched on.

"What a clever girl you are!" Sheridan clapped his hands. The little clock jingled enthusiastically.

"But how do we get back to the shop?" Letisha said. "Aren't we miles from where we came in?"

Mr Tempus held up his own Ouroboros by its little chain, his eyes twinkling. He flipped open the case, twiddled with the dials, and pointed the green beam that suddenly shot from the face at Letisha's little clock. It jumped a foot in the air in shock, before landing in the snow with a plop, its face glowing green. Letisha felt a slight tingle herself.

"What did you do?!" Letisha cried. "Poor thing!"

She rescued the little clock, but it wriggled free.

"I have given it some extra time," Mr Tempus took the clock, before pulling back his arm and hurling it into the air. "We might need back-up."

Letisha squealed and expected it to plummet to the ground below. Instead, it appeared to have caught the wind, and began to move away from them so fast it was quickly becoming a shooting star in the distance.

"What did you do that for?" she asked.

"Tempus Fugit," said Mr Tempus. "Time flies. Head for Bin Rist, bring Sigmund Adelinda and the clan!" he called out to the little clock, who stopped to look at them before shooting off with such speed Letisha struggled to focus on it for long.

"Right," Mr Tempus said firmly. "We need to get back to the Watch Room. Now, if I've designed the Ouroboros right, we should be able to get there on the double. Hang on a tick," He opened the watch to its third face. He adjusted several cogs, and nothing appeared to happen, until Letisha and Sheridan both realised how still the morning had become. In the distance, a flock of birds had halted in mid-air, and the wind had dropped.

"How long will it take you to get to Mule Root, Sheridan?"

"From here? Oh I don't know, a couple of hours, perhaps. Letisha is smaller now so I suppose she is easier to carry, but two passengers is difficult."

"We'll risk it," said Mr Tempus, as Sheridan crouched for them to get on. The morning stood completely still.

"Have you stopped time?" Letisha asked.

"No," Mr Tempus explained. "To all the people here, life goes on as normal. They have simply slowed down. Now, if I make a few more adjustments, I should be able to affect our time, so we are moving quadruply quick! Am I making sense?"

"Not in the slightest," said Sheridan, beginning to flap his wings. He was completely thrown as in a matter of seconds they were high in the air and Malice was miles behind them, though he felt as if he flapped at a normal speed. The speeding wind brought tears to his eyes.

"What did you do?" Sheridan cried.

"I simply arranged time around us. You don't spend over a century working as Father Time without learning a few tricks of the trade, you know. We should be at the portal in no time at all. Sheridan, do you know which door to go through? I haven't got a clue what it looks like from this end!"

"And make sure we don't come out in China!" Letisha said.

*

The little house on Covert Street began to rumble. Beneath the foundations of the shop, a great hoard of roots wound their way determinedly to the surface, thickening and hardening as they moved. They pushed through the soil like snakes through long grass, reaching for the light. Each driven by the same spirited force, the roots reached the solid foundations of the shop, as well as the foundations of the reality surrounding it, and prepared to burst through.

*

Sheridan approached the Portal Wall and touched down on the porch after mere minutes of flight. He stretched and folded his wings away, and Letisha adjusted her enormous clothes. She was now smaller than Mr Tempus, and held back behind him as he opened the door into his shop.
Mr Tempus tried to switch on a light, but found that the bulb had gone. Sheridan wrestled with a large cobweb that had stuck to his face as he ducked inside.

Letisha almost tripped over a discarded watch box as she entered, and sneezed as she realised that the floor was carpeted with dust. Gossamer cobwebs laced the walls, ceilings and rows of shelves. The faded room was a sorry sight.
Her feet echoed on the boards as she made her way into the front of the building. She decided to take a look outside before they faced the Watch Room.

The street was desolate; the windows broken in the houses, and the roofs crumbling into the buildings. The sky was grey and the trees were dead and black, their leaves fallen and blowing into the open doors of the houses.

There were no people, no birds singing. No cars drove by either. The silence was crushing. Letisha shivered.

"I've never seen a mortal street before," Sheridan remarked. "Quite a sorry sight, if you don't mind my saying."

"It's not normally like this!" Letisha cried. "Where is everyone?"

"This is what happens when the Architects fight. It has passed from the Otherworld and now our world is in discord too." Mr Tempus explained.

"My parents," Letisha cried. "My friends. What about them?"

"Be strong, Letisha," said Sheridan, placing a clawed hand on her little shoulder. "There have been many battles worse than this that have been won by the Adelinda Clan; I won't fail you."

"Come on," Mr Tempus said, as the empty street clearly unnerved him. "We have work to do."

Getting up the stairs proved to be a battle in itself. Most of the wood was rotten and broke as soon as Mr Tempus touched the bannister. Sheridan set one giant foot on the second step, having no use for the first. With a rumble, the staircase gave way all but for the last few steps at the top. They stood back as the dust and rubble settled, realising that the plaster on the walls was also crumbling. The floor had begun splitting under their feet.
Sheridan stood on his tiptoes, and stretched his body out as long as it would go, so that the tip of his nose was just a few inches shy of the landing.

"Quick, up my back," he cried, steadying himself against the cracking wall as Letisha and Mr Tempus clamoured up his rugged spine. Sheridan's grip began slipping as the bricks broke away in his hands. He giggled as something cold and firm slid under his belly, and around his feet and hands. Hoards of vines wound their way out of what was left of the floor and walls at incredible speed, growing up Sheridan's body and supporting him as they held the building together. They even grew around his nose, joining him to the landing and making a bridge for Letisha and Mr Tempus to safely climb across. After this, the vines pushed Sheridan onto the landing beside them, before retreating and mostly disappearing, save for filling in cracks and supporting the crumbling roof above their heads.
Letisha thought of Selena, back at Tempera-Sleus, before she turned and faced the door of the Watch Room with Mr Tempus and Sheridan. Behind it they heard the furious ticking of thousands of clocks.

Letisha took the Watch Room key from her pocket, and handed it to Mr Tempus. She knew he dreaded what he might find, for the Watch Room was no longer his.

27

MR DREAMSELLER REVEALED

Mr Tempus paused with the key in the door. He had crossed its threshold every night for longer than he cared to remember, but never with such fear in his heart. The situation did not bode well as they found the door to the Watch Room open.

Letisha followed him inside, along with Sheridan, who had to enter one limb at a time in order to fit. The house was losing its shape, and where the hallway seemed shorter, the doorway was bigger. It was as if the whole building was losing its grasp on reality, barely held together by the helpful vines.

Letisha stopped in her tracks behind Mr Tempus.

The room was now enormous, easily ten times the size she remembered it and at least twice as high. The beams buckled under the weight of the roof. There were more clocks than ever before, their ticking deafening. The floor stretched impossibly into blackness at the back of the room, but suddenly Letisha's attention was taken off these changes as she noticed that somebody was sitting at the workbench; he was impossibly tall, with a tall top hat on his head.

On their entry, Mr Dreamseller turned on the chair.

"Ah," he hissed, pressing his long fingers together. "I wasn't expecting guests."

Mr Tempus went rigid; Letisha couldn't see his face, but she pictured it frozen in fear. She also imagined determination in his quick eyes. She didn't understand why Mr Dreamseller was in the Watch Room.

"What's he doing here?" she whispered to Sheridan, but had her question answered as Mr Tempus spoke.

"Father Time," he said, "I have come for my son."

All three of them could see the bell jar containing Toby Tempus, only now he was conscious, watching them intently. His lips moved as he tried to speak, but the liquid obscured any sound.

Mr Dreamseller stood, his full and now terrifying height becoming clear. The tatty coat and trousers melted into red velvet robes, and his crooked hat drooped into a floppy affair atop his head. He smiled unnervingly, before taking up his Ouroboros, and pointing it at Letisha. In a flash, she found herself shooting backwards across the room and through the glass of the bell jar, where she became suspended in the green liquid. She was unable to even struggle as Sheridan raced forward to aid her. A group of wild nixies appeared out of nowhere to restrain him.

Mr Tempus was still rooted to the spot.

"Peter Tempus," Father Time boomed. "You and I have a lot to talk about."

*

Letisha opened her eyes to bright light and nothing else. She had expected to feel the coldness of the green liquid she had plummeted into. Instead, she was able to stand, and felt neither hot nor cold. She turned a full circle and could see nothing, nor could she gain any perspective. Somewhere she could hear voices echoing; one sounded like Mr Tempus, whereas the others were faint. She guessed they belonged to Sheridan and Father Time.

She may have been in a vast space, or indeed in a very small, bright cupboard. She could feel nothing beneath her feet, yet she did not fall. She called out to her friends, feeling utterly wretched for not being able to help on the brink of the battle. Her voice did not echo.

She jumped as somebody spoke behind her;

"Hullo,"

She turned to see a boy of about her own true age. He wore old-fashioned clothes; a white flannel shirt and trousers with braces. Concerned laced his face.

"Where am I?" Letisha said, still spinning and trying to feel for anything that might confirm she was not dead or dreaming. Here and there, the voices became clearer and then weaker, as if she were hearing them on the cusp of waking. In the distance, or possibly very close to her as she could not tell, shapes of moving people flashed. A large green shape struggled against many small blue ones, as Letisha felt as if the world was fading before her. The boy caught hold of her hands.

"You won't feel anything here, miss. There is nothing to feel. Although I can feel you so you must be real," he turned, as if he saw what she did. "Did he send you here too?

"Father Time sent me here. You're Toby, aren't you?"

The boy shook her hand as he continued to hold her, fascinated by the human contact.

"Tobias Tempus," he said, "Apprentice Watchmaker. And you are?"

"Letisha Tate," she said, "You're the one who's been writing on the mirror aren't you?

Toby's eyes grew wide. "I made contact! Do you know my father? Is he well?"

"He's fine. He's battling for your release. We need to get out of here!"

She freed herself from his grip and began to run around, looking for a wall to punch or a door to kick, but frustratingly found nothing. She swung her fist in the air and spun around pathetically, falling over. She felt as if she had not fallen at all, for she was once again standing beside Toby.

"It will do no good," he said. "Many a night I have watched my father sit alone, where I have touched his face, talked to him, but it never does any good. Sometimes I think he sees me for a moment, but then dismisses it. We are suspended, you and I."

Letisha sighed and ran her hand over her face. Toby was as lost and confused as she was.

"I thought you were a ghost," she admitted.

"I kept trying to talk to you when you were in my room. I didn't want you to touch my things."

"I didn't touch anything," Letisha snapped. "I didn't even want to stay in your room. Mr Tempus was convinced there was no ghost, but I suppose he doesn't feel you."

"No, he doesn't."

"A cruel trick on Time's part, no doubt," Letisha shrugged, ducking as the Sheridan-shaped colour managed to send a Nixie flying in front of her. The shapes were separate from them, and Letisha wondered how she looked from the outside. "So, how do we escape?"

*

"I suppose you think this will be simple," said Father Time, circling Mr Tempus like a wolf. In the corner, Sheridan could do nothing but watch, as the nixies securely froze to the floor.

"I've done my time," said Mr Tempus. "We had a deal; I owe you nothing more. Give me my son. Letisha has no value to you."

"I'll be the judge of that. I may have taken your son," said Father Time, finally standing still, "But do you have any idea what you took from me?"

As if on cue, a light blazed from the far end of the room and Jack Frost appeared, ushering forward Aunt Stackhouse. She whimpered in terror.

"You stole my immortal wife from me, upsetting the balance of the universe," Time went on. "You gave her a son, a disgusting abomination between mortal and Architect that should never have been. And when I stepped in and saved his life, you had to ruin everything.

"I know you have Jack's Ouroboros. Everything makes sense that you would have it; you were always asking questions. You reckoned it was because you're a collector. I always had my eye on you, Tempus. So, I'll cut you a deal. You return the Ouroboros to its rightful owner, and I don't kill Letisha and her dear aunt. Of course, if I do kill them, Jack Frost will be strong enough to find the Ouroboros himself. It's your choice."

Mr Tempus looked helplessly at the bell jar. "I don't have the Ouroboros anymore," he confessed. "And I don't know where it is." Father Time sighed and fiddled with the dials on his Ouroboros, pointing it at Aunt Stackhouse. A faint green glow appeared about his hand, but disappeared as Mr Tempus cried out.

"Wait! What if I could give you something better than his Ouroboros? A Fourth Ouroboros. I confess; I did some research, and from what you taught me about the Watch Room and the ways of Time I built my own. And it works, too. It is completely pure, too young to be corrupt by years of bitterness and jealousy, and not bound to one owner. Made by mortal hands, it is infinitely special. And infinitely powerful."

"Look at that!" murmured Jack Frost, rubbing his spindly hands together. "I could use one of those. My old Ouroboros always was a bit clunky." He dragged poor Aunt Stackhouse with him as he came closer to Mr Tempus to get a better look at the watch. The air became noticeably icier as he approached. He tried to touch the Fourth Ouroboros but Mr Tempus quickly snatched it away.

"Look with your eyes, friend. My quarrel is not with you." Father Time was so angry that his face turned the same colour as his robes. He stormed up to Mr Tempus, forcing Jack Frost to sidestep out of the way.

"You mean to tell me a mortal, a scrubby little know-nothing mortal, managed to build something equal to that most precious and powerful of gifts given to the three Architects that gave birth to the entire universe? We imagined you, Peter Tempus, we built you, and you replicated the very machine that created you? You expect me to believe that?"

"You seem to believe I stole your wife," said Mr Tempus, pocketing the Ouroboros. "I think you'll believe anything."

"I believe I will destroy you," growled Father Time, preparing his Ouroboros. Jack Frost looked equally nervous and annoyed; he was tempted by the new Ouroboros and didn't want to see it obliterated.

28

THE DRAGONS DESCEND

The mornings' peace was shattered as hundreds of beating wings carried almost the entire Adelinda clan across the reddening sky towards Mule-Root. At the head of the v-shaped formation, Uncle Sigmund donned his best flying goggles, as well as a leather aviator hat especially adapted for his horns. Behind him, the puff thundered at a tremendous speed, the low clouds gliding over their scaled bodies. Some of them chatted politely as they moved along; the whole event would be a talking point for years to come.

Uncle Sigmund had his reservations about visiting the little shop on the other side of the Portal Wall, but since the little clock had arrived with such gusto – shooting right through the glass in the front window – rallying the clan and moving quickly seemed like the only thing to do.

They would reach the wall in no time at all going at maximum speed. Uncle Sigmund carried the little clock, buttoned firmly into the pocket of his waistcoat.

As they drew in and the wall loomed, the dragons began to pick up speed; it would take a great force to burst into the oncoming battle.

*

Letisha paced back and forth as she helplessly watched the confrontation. The atmosphere of the Watch Room was leaking into the bell jar, cooling the air sufficiently.

Toby Tempus watched curiously; he seemed to have resigned himself to an existence in this white space. He jumped, suddenly noticing a cool breeze, something he hadn't felt for a long time.

"Where's that cold coming from?" he asked.

"It's Jack Frost," she said. "If only I could break through that glass and free us both…" She considered removing one of her prized boots and simply bashing away at the air until she had some luck.

"I haven't felt the wind in so long." Toby muttered distantly. He held out his hands and let the mysterious breeze blow through his fingers. It was so strong that it moved Letisha's hair as hundreds of tiny dandelion seeds blew towards Toby.

"My favourites," he whispered.

Letisha narrowed her eyes. She was certain she hadn't been in this place very long but everything she understood about it meant that the breeze didn't make sense. Nothing in the world outside would be producing such an effect. She was confused to say the least, as the white space pulsed blue, then green, and something cold wound its way around her ankles and wrists. She gave out a small cry, but then saw that the same thing was happening to Toby; four green vines wound their way around his wrists and ankles, before sweeping him backwards and pulling him out of the whiteness with a pop.

"Toby?" Letisha cried. A second later, she felt herself rushing backwards too. She closed her eyes tightly against a great surge of hot and cold all at once.

*

Letisha and Toby were brought back into reality covered in the remnants of the Time they had been held in with a crash. They rolled across the floor and landed neatly beside Sheridan with a plop, scattering baffled nixies in all directions. Anything that wasn't moving quickly enough was covered with tickers.

As a blaze of green light left Father Time's Ouroboros in the direction of Mr Tempus, there was a flash, and the power that surged from his weapon froze in mid-air. It then fell to the floor and shattered like glass, as another figure entered the room unannounced.

From her shelter beside Sheridan, Letisha studied the woman who had appeared to save Mr Tempus.

She had the same sort of air about her as Selena, only she had hair as red as lava, and robes of dark green, laced with a pattern of fine ivy. She held an Ouroboros of her own, and another dangled from her belt. Letisha knew she was looking at Selena, Mr Tempus's long lost wife, and Mother Earth, all one and the same.

"Your quarrel is not with these mortals," she said in a gentle voice that somehow roared with all the power of an earthquake.

"Mother Earth," Father Time grinned mockingly. "I do believe I forgot to invite you to our little party. Still, you know everyone, so I don't have to introduce you."

"Mother Earth?" Letisha whispered to Sheridan. "That's Mother Earth?"

"Anna?" Mr Tempus managed. "How is this possible?"

She turned and looked at Mr Tempus, her face softening. She took the Ouroboros from her belt, and tossed it to Jack Frost. He shoved Aunt

Stackhouse out of the way and flipped it open, only to find the little vial empty; there was no time in his Ouroboros.

He looked up at Mother Earth, his eyes glowing a ferocious arctic blue.

"You! You used up all the Time in this! How am I supposed to recover now?!"

"You fool," she said. "You wasted your own time and you gave away this most precious gift to pursue something that could never be yours. Now look where it has landed you; you're a disgusting skeleton of your former self, driven only by your selfishness."

Father Time's anger towards Mr Tempus was temporarily snuffed as he regarded his former wife and the Architect who had spent so much time trying to win her.

Jack Frost very nearly froze the room with his rage; breath danced out of the mouths of those who didn't hold it; even the nixies stopped trying to attack Letisha and Toby and watched to see what would happen. The shining shells of the Tickers frosted up, too.

"I can fill this up again," said Jack Frost, and turned towards Aunt Stackhouse, bent on having her time for his own. He pointed his Ouroboros as he twisted the cogs menacingly with his long cold fingers. "Your time will soon be mine."

Suddenly, Jack Frost froze where he stood. He gave a small, bewildered croak as smoky hands twisted their way around him, one even snaking through his chest. The misty tendrils held him fast. At his shoulder, the bitter face of Mrs Grisham's Ghost appeared in the grey smog as she whispered in a chilling voice,

"You should have known I'd find you one day, Frosty Jack Grisham."

As she said this, Jack Frost's face tightened and grew immensely pale. He became transparent, his hair thinned and fell, and his eyes grew wide in his skull. Mrs Grisham's Ghost surrounded him, consumed him, as he became thinner and more ghostly even than she.

The room watched in horror as the mighty but foolish Architect was reduced to nothing more than essence within his wife's clutches. His golden Ouroboros fell to the ground with a dull clank. Like a wisp of smoke blown from an extinguished candle, all that remained of him fell perfectly into the movements of the watch, before it snapped itself shut, and they were both gone.

29

FIRE AND ICE

Father Time gawped at the dull Ouroboros as it lay dead and useless on the Watch Room floor. He glared at Mother Earth with an almost baffled expression, until he remembered himself and drew his Ouroboros on her. This time, a red light crawled through the air made its way towards her and she became captured within its power. To everyone's surprise, she produced an identical green light that did the same, and they both struggled in one another's grip, each drawing the other closer, waltzing to a rhythm nobody else heard. They partially faded from the fabric of the room, just as there came the splintering of wood and the tumbling of tiles, along with a deafening clatter. The roof of the little building was torn off, and through the gaping hole came an enormous Puff of dragons led by Uncle Sigmund, roaring ferociously. Red dragons with silver bellies attacked the nixies on entry, melting them away to nothing. A number of odd dragons covered with wispy silver-white hair struck out at the Tickers, shattering their bodies effortlessly.

Letisha suspected that Mother Earth and Father Time were now fighting where she and Toby had been imprisoned, despite the bell jar being shattered. She remembered this as she felt something crumble under her feet; Mother Earth was apparently strong enough to break Otherworld Glass. She saw an impression of them move and shimmer in a mixture of red and green, around and through the racks loaded with clocks, jingling with fear.

Tearing herself away from watching the battle, Letisha herded Toby away from various flying debris. They crawled away from the conflict and sought shelter in a corner of the room. Mr Tempus shielded them from the fighting with his tiny body. Toby was in a state of shock, as he barely registered that he was squatting next to his father. Aunt Stackhouse was still shaken by her close encounter with Jack Frost, almost too dazed to shield herself from the onslaught.
More and more nixies and tickers emerged to battle with the dragons, who kept coming in their droves, diving in from the night sky above them as the Otherworld and the Mortal World collided.
As Letisha batted a number of smaller Tickers off her coat, she wondered which world they were even in, since a group of dragons crashing through

the roof of a little shop in a country village would cause a sensation if they were spotted. The noise was tremendous.

She jumped as she felt a nudge at her side, and the little purple clock jumped and jingled with joy at seeing her. She clutched it close and ducked, as the splash of a melted Nixie hit the wall above them, and the battle between fire and ice ensued.

Mother Earth and Father Time had managed to separate themselves from the rest of the room. They glided on another plane, sometimes passing through other bodies unnoticed, though their forms became visible once in a while. Now that Letisha was fully aware that she had previously met Mother Earth at home and at Tempera-Sleus. Sheridan had known her for years and been none the wiser. Just how many disguises she might wear in order to keep her identity a secret was baffling.

She also concluded that the reason Selena had been so involved was because she was Mother Earth, as old as Time and Frost, all knowing in every sense. Suddenly she realised that she had met fewer people in the Otherworld than she first believed; the Architects were fond of disguises.

Just inches away from Sheridan's foot, the dead Ouroboros belonging to Jack Frost began to twitch slightly, as though he were attempting escape.

Sheridan slapped his hand onto it, pulling it out of the way of the twirling Architects. He wrapped the chain tightly around the watch, before stuffing it into his pocket.

"Oh no you don't," he said firmly, and ducked as Mother Earth's staff swung out, missing his head by only a hair's distance.

Father Time was now determined; his wife had betrayed him for the last time, and he would be done with her once and for all. If he couldn't have her, nobody could, and he swung his own staff, reserved for special occasions, such as the destruction of another Architect.

She ducked and twirled like a feather on the breeze, slamming her staff into his chest, where the orb flashed blue for a second. His robes cushioned the blow slightly, but he still staggered back before lunging at her once more. He struck not her upper body but her legs, sending her toppling to the floor

"I killed you once before," he reminded her. "I can easily do it again."

She was not wounded, but biding her time, and jabbed the butt of her staff into his right knee before flipping to her feet once more. He howled in pain as she said, "Anna Tempus was mortal. Even Jack Frost can kill a mortal."

"What did that spirit do to him?" he said, spinning his weapon in the air before attempting to bring it down on her head, and missing. "A spirit can't kill an Architect,"

"Hell hath no fury like a woman scorned," she said, ducking back as he missed her again. He was taller than her and slightly gangly, whereas she was fluid and graceful. "I don't imagine Jack Frost is dead, but I doubt he is little more than the very essence of the seasons. Are you telling me you don't think he deserved that?"

"Everyone makes mistakes," said Father Time, spinning unnaturally quickly and striking a blow in her back.

"A mistake is made by accident," she said, wincing as he dealt her another blow to the chest.

"Any man who marries is making a mistake," Time spat, trying to catch his breath. "I don't see proposing as accidental in the slightest. If you had not cast him off in the first place he would never have settled for marrying a mortal. Her death is your fault."

"I would never have left you for Frost, however much he begged me," Mother Earth replied venomously. "I found a mortal man better than either of you."

Time seethed, as he received a painful crack to the ribs. He felt something split, but would make time to fix it later.

Mother Earth's eyes glowed gold, as she knew he was struggling. He may have stolen the form of a younger man, but he was still ancient. She knew that no matter what tricks he played or taunts he threw at her, a minute would still be sixty seconds long, and a day would still have twenty-four hours in it. On the other hand, no two trees would ever be the same, nor would any two fingerprints; she was as free as she had ever been, as was her power.

Father Time was weakening. Though he still stood, he clutched his ribs awkwardly, trying not to show pain. They may have been Architects but there were elements that were still so fragile and human. He had been damaged since she had left, and it still hurt. She hurt too, thanks to his selfishness.

"You and I aren't so different," she said, preparing to counter his attack. She enjoyed giving him a good telling off.

He looked up at her with his staff ready to strike, but also his Ouroboros in the other hand as she spoke. He noticed the hoards of green and brown vines that cracked through the floor and walls of the Watch Room, slithering amongst the battling nixies and dragons, weaving their way around his feet. He took for granted that they would not enter their battle.

"We both have selfish drives, Father," said Mother Earth, her face unmoving as the vines continued to weave. "Had I not left you for a mortal man, you would have left me sooner or later, for you are a fickle creature.

You may still have your Ouroboros, but you have given away your Watch Room, your robes and your knowledge. You chose to live the life of a drifter while a poor mortal did your work for you. You might have banished me and taken my mortal body, but I am still working. I work to to make the sun and the moon rise, and the earth grow and move. The leaves in the trees blow to the rhythm of my breath, every spirit lives to my blueprint. I know when to be cruel, where you are cruel for your own selfish gains,"

As she said this, the vines that pulsed with blue lights wound their way up the spindly legs of Father Time, and around his broken torso, securing his arms in tight, squeezing them so that he could no longer hold his staff.

In the struggle, Time finally lost the grip on his beloved Ouroboros. It fell from his grasp, the chain running through his fingers, though he still failed to grab it. It clattered pathetically to the floor.

At this point, Mother Earth turned to the mortals, cowering out of the way. She knew what needed to be done.

30

AS IT SHOULD BE

Fighting every instinct to keep her head down, Letisha looked up and noticed that the gap between the two realities was thinning. Mother Earth was bringing the battles together.

Time was bound in a coil of vines so tight his eyes were bulging. Through the ropier vines and the new ones that continued to twist around him, his expression burned with unparalleled rage.

Mother Earth looked satisfied with her work. She spoke in a very calm voice.

"Hand me the Fourth Ouroboros, Letisha."

Mr Tempus shakily took out the watch and handed it to Letisha, who held it out to Mother Earth. She looked at the flat and seemingly useless object in the palm of Letisha's hand. She then looked to Father Time, enraged and still trying to fight his way out of a cage that was struggling to hold him.

Without really knowing what she was doing, Letisha tossed the Fourth Ouroboros into the air, where it stopped mid-flight, along with everything else going on around them. Three nixies that had climbed onto the back of Uncle Sigmund and were about to be burned by one of his clan were paused even as they melted, the water drops suspended from their shimmering bodies like diamonds. A floorboard that had cracked beneath the feet of a particularly large dragon whose neck and chest shimmered with chainmail, had simply stopped, little chips of wood flying up in all directions paused in their paths. Only Letisha, Mother Earth and Father Time were able to look around, though every pair of eyes in the room was on them. Father Time was struggling, his head now bound nearly still with pulsing vines.

With no more than a blink of Mother Earth's golden eyes, the Fourth Ouroboros split open as if it had hit the ground, and the three faces separated, as did all the elements themselves. Cogs of all sizes spread out between the faces, and lined up like planets in orbit. The vial of green time hovered too, until Mother Earth reached out, took it, and held it between her delicate fingers. Father Time tried to speak but more vines muffled his voice.

"Time is a funny thing," she said. "It can be given, taken, spent and saved, but all too often, it is simply wasted. Wouldn't you agree, Letisha?"

Letisha nodded, transfixed by the frozen watch parts.

"I have wasted Time," Mother Earth admitted. "I should have tried to save Peter Tempus and our son from this cruelty a long time ago, even though Time ensured I was tooo weak. I knew Peter didn't remember me, but he remembered our son. There was still something in Peter that knew I would help wherever I could. That's why I hid the Fourth Ouroboros from this idiot for safekeeping. Were you not brave enough to rescue my husband, I might never have seen him or my son again.

"Now," she said, tipping her head at Father Time. "What do you think we should do with this tyrant?"
Letisha thought for a moment. She looked back at Mr Tempus and Toby and then at Sheridan, frozen as he clutched the little purple clock. She smiled as she had a marvellous idea.

"You can't destroy an Architect, can you?"

"I'm afraid not," Mother Earth shook her head. "We are the pillars of the Universe."

"Mr Tempus has a saying about this place," said Letisha. "What happens in the Watch Room stays in the Watch Room."
Mother Earth smiled, a genuine, heartfelt smile. She understood Letisha perfectly.

"What an imaginative suggestion." Mother Earth turned to Father Time. "My dear, I could never destroy you. We built this place together, and you were so proud of it; I never thought you would give it away. It is time for you to start work again, and this workshop shall be your prison."
With that, she threw the vial of time in the direction of her husband. It spun in slow motion at first, as everything began to catch up with itself. Finally it hit him at full speed, and all too soon he was nothing but a green haze. Vines disappeared between the frozen gears and cogs of the Forth Ouroboros, as the parts began to snap back together. Time sped up too fast for Letisha's comfort, as the Ouroboros hit the floor with a thud, and the wood began to splinter and disintegrate around them. Nixies shrieked and melted through the boards, while the dragons took to their wings as they were sucked out of the shattered roof above into a starless sky too dark to be real.

In a trice the outer walls of the Watch Room were gone, and only pieces of the floor remained, where the mortals clung desperately to the supporting beams to avoid being thrown over the threshold.
In the middle of it all, Mother Earth still stood as her spell took effect and the Watch Room was no longer hidden in the broom cupboard of a little terraced house, but imprisoned within the gears and cogs of a watch, a prison their master was powerless to resist. Letisha clung to Mother Earth's robes desperately as a violent wind whipped around her face. A splinter of wood

gave her a cut across her exposed cheek. She screamed in pain, though nobody heard. A whirlwind consumed everything around them; the Watch Room was rapidly disappearing.

Then there was silence. Despite the blood trickling down her cheek, Letisha saw no stain on Mother Earth's robes as she dared to pull her face away. Around her, the night was peaceful, if not eerily quiet, and she realised how high up they were.

She looked around, still holding the robes for support. She could see for miles, for they were high above the town. Daylight shone on the streets below. Above them a void loomed, so black and heavy Letisha felt that she might be crushed. It was the same kind of blackness she had fallen into when she had tumbled off the patio.

As she remembered this Letisha dared not creep too close to the edge of the precipice. From a distance, she imagined the building might have looked as though the topmost portion had simply been lopped clean off with an axe. Save for one surviving corner the square floor space was completely exposed. The floorboards were all but gone in the centre of the room. The edges were battered and buckling, but still managed to support their weight.

"What happens now?" Letisha whispered. "What happens to the town?"

"Everything must go back as it should be," said Mother Earth. She pointed to the sky. "This is what happens when a portalfrom our world to yours is destroyed. Father Time kept his Watch Room in several places, but I imagine mostly he was keeping an eye on Mr Tempus."

"Where are we?"

Mother Earth looked around as she walked to the edge of the structure. The ground was a dizzying distance below. She cast no shadow as the blackness overhead began to shrink and heal itself.

Letisha looked around too, and recognised the yellow stone of the building.

"This is the church," she said. "Well, it was."

"The clock tower, naturally," said Mother Earth. She raised her hands and the void above them healed over, as the sun rose in the distance, casting a brilliant golden light over the sleeping town. Behind them, a little voice spoke.

"Anna?"

Letisha and Mother Earth turned, and Letisha gasped, as she realised that the remainder of her companions were still huddled in a corner of the clock tower that had somehow survived. Toby, Sheridan and Aunt Stackhouse were quite intact, as was Uncle Sigmund, who had been clinging to the side of the building like a bat.

Mr Tempus however, was not the man he had been. He sat up, his long legs dangling into the crevasse. He had a long torso, clad in a white shirt, and a kind handsome face topped with a crop of thick brown hair. Letisha recognised him as being the man she had come to know as Mr Dreamseller, only he was different now; he had softened. As he stood, and walked precariously around the edge of the broken clock tower, she saw that his mannerisms were familiar; he had a little twist and a jaunt to his step.

He walked confidently up to them, staring into the face of Mother Earth as if he had seen a ghost. She smiled softly as he put his hand to her cheek, and whispered,

"You were dead."

"Only mortally," she said. "I never did tell you what I did for a living, did I, Peter?"

31

BACK TO REALITY

Uncle Sigmund and Sheridan ensured that everyone got to the ground safely, offering lifts from the remains of the church.

Toby, who had never seen a dragon before an entire puff had burst through the ceiling of the Watch Room, had to be coaxed onto Sheridan's back in order to reach the ground. He was still in shock.

Letisha and Aunt Stackhouse were the last people left on the roof. Sheridan offered a hand to Aunt Stackhouse, who shook violently inside her baggy cardigan. Her glowering eyes stretched wide, and her expression was nothing short of ghastly.

Aunt Stackhouse shook her head rigidly, where Sheridan shrugged and descended from the ruins with Letisha clinging on for dear life. She doubted she would ever tell anyone at home that she had sat on a dragons' back as he jumped off the ruined bell tower of a church.

Mother Earth was concerned when Letisha and Sheridan landed without her grim aunt in tow.

"She wont get on," Letisha shrugged. "I think it's all been too much for her. I'll be in so much trouble if she tells my parents about this."

"Well, that's not going to happen," Mother Earth sighed. Apparently she sometimes forgot just how stubborn mortals could be.

"How can you be sure?" Letisha cried.

"Oh, call it a knack for understanding people," Mother Earth winked. She glanced up at the precipice from where Aunt Stackhouse now watched them, rolled her eyes, and then banged her staff on the dewy grass.

Letisha blinked, and her aunt was standing beside her. Letisha gasped, and was about to beg the old crone not to breathe a word of what she had seen, when Aunt Stackhouse shrieked. It was a long, wild shriek one would expect more from a banshee than a grown woman.

"You, Letisha Tate, belong in a circus!" she cried, just about managing to form a sentence between screams. "You and all the rest of these... these... hideous creatures!"

Sheridan and Uncle Sigmund gasped, clearly offended.

"And don't you even think about asking to come and stay with me when your parents go gadding off again!"

"Now, Liz…none of this is Letisha's fault…" Mr Tempus tried to step in. He placed an arm around Letisha's shoulders as she looked as if she was about to cry.

"And you. I don't know who you are or what happened to the real Mr Tempus, but you'd better believe I'd report this whole disaster to the proper authorities if they wouldn't throw me in the madhouse for it!"

With that, she stormed off into the morning. Mr Tempus held onto Letisha, though she had no intention of going after her aunt anyway.

With Aunt Stackhouse thundering away into the morning, Mother Earth began to confess her story.

"You might as well know," she drew a deep breath. "I am Anna Tempus, or I was a long time ago. I came to the mortal world to hide from my duties, before Time destroyed my mortal body and sent me back. He and Jack Frost slowly added more doors and Portals to the wall on the edge of Mule Root in order to make my return to the shop impossible. I knew if I did anything drastic Toby would be jeopardised.

"And that little charm to make you forget me worked a treat," Anna said sadly, still unable to believe she was standing beside her husband. "It was only by chance that Sheridan and his uncle happened across the shop. Sigmund knew me as Selena, and I fed bits of the story from time to time as merely hearsay."

"But what about the Ouroboros?" asked Mr Tempus. "My Ouroboros."

"I didn't like to take it from you," Mother Earth admitted. "But I knew since I gave you the book you might try to replicate it. What man who is fascinated by the art of saving time wouldn't? When I did find the shop, I took the Ouroboros and hid it within the pages of the book. That way it wouldn't leave the shop and it wouldn't be easily accessed either, and certainly not without magic."

Letisha felt as if it had all happened too easily. Though she saw the Fourth Ouroboros in the hand of Mother Earth, she thought that it might be too simple for somebody as strong and apparently power mad as Father Time to escape its clutches.

Her thoughts were disturbed as she noticed something glimmer in the wet grass, a few feet from where she stood. She walked over and stooped to pick up a small locket on a chain. She let it dangle and spin, until she opened it and recognised the picture.

"Mrs Grisham's Ghost!" she cried.

The rest of the party turned around in panic, but Mr Tempus smiled and pointed to the smoky white figure standing beside Letisha. Mrs Grisham's Ghost wore a clean white dress, and her hair was wound up neatly atop her head. She glowed and smiled softly, which made Letisha struggle to realise who she was until she spoke.

"You can cast that thing to the rubbish heap."

"Mrs Grisham's Ghost?" Letisha gasped

"Ghost no longer, my child. I am avenged at last, and I can move on."

"But your search, your husband…"

"I am more without that scoundrel, and I will waste no more of my afterlife searching for him. Besides, I have a new gentleman friend."

Beside her, another figure appeared. He wore white military clothes and was mostly bald, but he was clean and primped, and glowed.

"Duke?" Letisha gasped.

"Yes, my dear girl," he said.

"I'm so sorry, this is all my fault, if you hadn't come with us to Malice you might still be alive!"

"I would gladly die for an adventure!" admitted the spirit of Nelson, Duke of Quill. "And now, with the afterlife ahead of me, I have a whole new adventure to begin. Take my arm, my dear Una."

Mrs Grisham's Ghost took his arm, giggling like a schoolgirl. They both began to glow brighter.

"Thank you, Letisha Tate," they whispered, before their voices faded out, and they were gone.

Letisha did as she was told, almost, and dug a small hole in which she buried the locket holding the picture of Jack Frost.

"Well done, Letisha," said Uncle Sigmund, removing his goggles and laying a hand on her shoulder. "Well done."

Mother Earth held her son's and husband's hands, and looked up at the devastated church.

"Such a shame. I happen to love churches. It is time to put things right," said Mother Earth.

She took out her Ouroboros, opened it, and pointed it at the building. While the onlookers watched, the church began to rebuild itself from the debris about the yard, with bits of timber, brick and tile moving themselves back into place securely, until the church was good as new again. It was beautiful with the glow of the sunrise on its eastern face. The clock told them that the hour was six, but it did not tick.

"Time will heal before long," said Mr Tempus on seeing the stopped clock.

"I don't think I'll ever get used to you like this," Letisha admitted.

"You didn't think I was always an old man, did you?" he chuckled. "When I bargained with Father Time, he took my life and my youth, and I took his old body. This is my true face. It's much better, don't you think?"

"It's wonderful," Letisha said, clutching the little purple clock.

Mother Earth knelt, facing Letisha.

"I am sorry Letisha, but for things to go back as they should be, you will have to bid farewell to your friends. But first, I think I owe you a couple of years."

She pointed her Ouroboros at Letisha, who felt the floor becoming further away and her clothes tighten. Her boots fit her once more. She patted her body, and realised that she was once again eleven-year-old Letisha Tate. She was quite happy too, as she believed that Mother Earth might have even made her a little taller. She ran to Sheridan and hugged him.

"Goodbye, Sheridan. You're the best friend a girl could ever ask for. Here," she handed the little clock over to him. "I want you to take care of this little chap; he'll be safe with you.

Sheridan wailed and dabbed his eyes with his tail.

"I'll never forget you, my dear little Letisha!"

Uncle Sigmund squeezed them both as he temporarily let his emotions get the better of him.

"We'll keep that little clock wound up, and you'll never be late again!"

Letisha turned to Mr Tempus and Toby.

"Thank you for taking care of me, Mr Tempus. High school doesn't seem so daunting now; I think I can take on anything!"

Mother Earth steeled herself, surrounded by her family and two dragons – one sobbing and one trying not to – and pointed the Ouroboros at Letisha. She took one last look at her friends before she felt time stand still and speed up all at once. She had the sensation of being swept backwards, and the morning faded to bright white.

32

AN EXCEPTIONAL KEEPER OF TIME

Letisha opened her eyes, expecting to hear the sound of the alarm, but found that she had woken at seven 'o'clock sharp without needing any help. She sat up rubbing her eyes, and looked out of the window to a beautiful summer morning.

In the kitchen, her mother was rushing around, putting the last bits into her carry-on bag, saying that they were going to be late. There was still more than forty minutes before they were due to go out.

Letisha knew it was the day her mother was due to fly to Bahamas only because of the calendar. She ate her breakfast in confusion, trying to convince herself that she was not dreaming.

"Mum," she began slowly, rinsing her bowl and spoon on the sink. "Have I been away recently?"

"What?" Mum asked in confusion. "We went to Devon over half term. Don't you remember?"

"No, I mean recently. In the last week."

"Oh Letisha, you are so full of whimsy, sometimes." Mum decided to change the subject. "I think finishing school has been a big strain on you. Still, about packing your bag..."

"I'm sorting it now!" Letisha cried. "I've had other things on my mind!"

"What do you mean?" said Mrs Tate, pointing to Letisha's suitcase, nestled beside the other luggage. "I was most impressed you'd got it packed already. I didn't think you'd be so enthusiastic to stay with Mr Tempus, but then you always did get on with young Toby, didn't you?"

Letisha narrowed her eyes, and tried not to fall over as memories came rushing back to her. She saw a boy of about her age, and his parents in a house she didn't visit often enough. It was as if she had known the Tempus family all her life, while living another life alongside. Her memories of the past week were unaltered.

Letisha considered sharing this sudden rush of recollections with her mother, but decided against it. Mum was far too busy to worry about her bizarre fantasies.

After riding on the back of a dragon, being inside a car was weird enough, as well as having her mother beside her.

"You said I'd met Mr Tempus before," Letisha tried to prompt her mother into talking. "But I'm not sure I remember him at all."

Mum wasn't listening, too preoccupied with the traffic.

"You're not worried about what I might get up to while you're away?" Letisha went on.

Mum sighed. "I always forget what a trek this is."

Letisha was no longer concerned about being so far from home without her parents. She had slept in a dragon's house and a witches' hideaway, so a comfortable bed in a slightly creepy house didn't seem so bad.

"I really haven't seen Mr Tempus recently?" Letisha asked.

"I daresay you'll feel right at home in a watchmaker's." Mum continued as if Letisha wasn't even talking.

"What do you mean? You always said the clock was my worst enemy!"

"Nonsense," Mum went on. "Everyone knows my daughter is the most punctual creature in the universe. Look, here's the turning!"

Letisha hung onto the door for dear life as her mother screeched onto a little side road at the last minute. Once, she would have been nervous about visiting a new place, but she had travelled this road recently; she knew exactly where she was going.

They left the car on a small car park with no tarmac and walked half the length of the single street village to find the shop. The road was adorned with silver birch trees and little green benches dotted with pensioners and ramblers.

They reached the end of the narrow lane. A house on the left had a little sign hanging above the door. In beautifully hand painted script were the words 'P. Tempus, Master Watchmaker'.

They stopped outside, where Mum sighed and turned to Letisha. "You do look smart, Letisha."

Letisha had no answer to that, so her mother continued.

"Have you got your watch on?"

"What?"

Mum sighed and pulled out a box from her handbag, holding a watch that Letisha recognised immediately; with a plain silver casing and small chain attached. Mrs Tate removed it from the box and fixed it to the inside of

Letisha's coat, before placing into the breast pocket. It was slightly warm against her.

"I think you've earned this," said Mum firmly. Letisha made no response, still baffled. They hugged, before Letisha noticed the time on her mothers watch.

"You're going to be late, Mum."

"Oh drat," Mum sighed. "Well, let me come in with you at least…"

"I'll be alright. I can keep myself out of trouble for a few weeks."

"Well, if you're sure…" Mum sounded slightly concerned at her daughters' newfound independence.

"I'm sure," Letisha kissed Mum's cheek.

"Oh. Well then, pass my regards to the family, won't you. I'll see you soon, Letisha. We love you very much."

"Bye Mum," Letisha said quietly, hugging her mother again, before she turned and headed back towards the car park, leaving Letisha alone with her suitcase.

*

Letisha entered the shop nervously, unsure of what she might find; the last time she saw it, it was falling apart. To her delight the little shop was alive with the sound of ticking.

"Is that you, Letisha?" came a voice from behind the counter.
Letisha jumped and looked to the gap in the worktop. Looking over at her smiling, there was possibly the tallest man she had ever laid eyes on. He had a familiar face and bright blue eyes that twinkled as if he knew the world's greatest secret.

"Mr Tempus!" she cried, and leapt forward to hug him. "I thought I'd never see you again."

He smiled. "I've been waiting for you, you know."
She began to speak when the front door jingled, and a boy she also recognised entered. Again memories came flooding back. Toby Tempus took up an apron from the counter and handed it to her.

"You'll be sharing my duties as apprentice watchmaker."

"Nonsense, Toby," said another voice, soft yet stern. Letisha gasped as a woman appeared behind Mr Tempus, with long red hair wound into a tight plait. She wore a green suit whose edges were adorned with gold, and a large watch hung from her belt. Anna Tempus was just as beautiful in her human form. "You'll be working just as hard to help Letisha in the shop."

"I…but…you…." Letisha just about managed to speak. She looked from Mr Tempus to his wife, then to his son, and then back to Mr Tempus. It was as if she had known them all her life.

"Letisha, you remember Toby, and my wife, Anna."
Letisha was still genuinely speechless.

"Didn't I say," Anna Tempus began, her eyes flashing from blue to green to gold. "That everything would go back as it should be? And how are you taking care of that Ouroboros for us?"
Letisha took the watch from her pocket, suddenly realising what it was, and who was imprisoned inside it.

"But…why me?" Letisha asked.

"Who else better to take care of such an important watch than a most exceptional keeper of time?" said Mr Tempus. He stopped as a mighty knock came from the back door. "Toby, would you get that please?"

In the stock room, Toby turned the huge key, and just about managed to pull open the colossal back door.
Letisha was delighted as she set eyes on an enormous pair of green clawed feet, a belly that glimmered like mother of pearl, a very smart waistcoat, and grinning jaws full of sparkling teeth.

"Oh glory of glories!" exclaimed Sheridan, racing into the shop and clutching Letisha so tightly she gasped. He gave no care to who might see him from the street. "You're finally here!"
She pulled herself free of his enthusiastically tight grip.

"It's good to see you, Sheridan. How is everything?"

"Everything is fabulous! Uncle is well and has his hands full with our new little clock, thanks to you!" He giggled and clapped his hands. "And now, I have two little friends to take on adventures with me!"

"Not so fast, Sheridan," said Anna sternly. "Toby and Letisha have work to do."

"That's right," Letisha said. "If Aunt Stackhouse comes in and sees me messing about with you lot she'll have a heart attack."

"I don't think so," Mr Tempus cut in. "I don't think we'll have to worry about her bothering us anymore."

"Is this something else I'll remember eventually?" Letisha moaned.

"You don't remember her calling me a hideous creature and saying we all belonged in a circus?" Sheridan cried. "I was most offended."

Anna grinned. "I didn't think your aunt needed any more incentive to leave you alone than remembering everything. She knows what might happen if she tries to make trouble for you again."

Letisha's jaw dropped. "But…what if she tells somebody? What if the police come banging on the door and asking…wait a minute," she paused for a moment to catch up. "Nobody will believe her, will they?"

"Not in a million years," Toby chuckled.

"So the past has changed?" Letisha tried to get her head around everything.

"It didn't exactly change," Anna explained. "It just split in half; changed enough that we could be together, but still have you in the equation. There are now two versions of our history, but we have the favourable outcome. We do want you around, Letisha, especially since you have somebody very important in your safekeeping."

Nervously, Letisha put her hand in her pocket and retrieved the Fourth Ouroboros. She shrieked and dropped it only a moment later, as it had become scorching hot in her hands. It vibrated against the boards and sizzled the wood where it lay, as if its captive was very, very angry.

"Oh, do stop it," Anna snapped at the watch. She nudged it with her foot and the vibrating ceased. "He might complain once in a while, but you just have to be firm with him."

"Oh," Letisha said. "So he's not gone then?"

"By no means," Anna said, retrieving the rapidly cooling Ouroboros. "We felt that you would be best at taking care of him. That thing isn't going to fall into the hands of anyone that can use it in this world."

"Don't look so glum," Sheridan patted her shoulder. "I have Jack Frost to contend with!" He took Jack Frost's Ouroboros out of his pocket. As he did, the surface of the watch frosted up. "He's got a nasty temper, I can tell you!"

"We don't need to worry about either of them, Letisha," Mr Tempus rolled his eyes. Letisha knew he didn't even want to contemplate what might happen if either prisoner escaped. "You'll be too busy helping Toby adjust to the twenty-first century to worry about Time."

"I can manage," Toby said defensively.

"Enough chit chat!" Sheridan clapped his hands as if directing a performance. "Mr Tempus, you promised I could take them out. You promised!"

"Yes, Father. You told me yourself!" Toby said, pulling on his coat as if the decision were already made. His mother simply smiled, and Letisha could see how truly glad she was to be home.

Mr Tempus sighed in mock defeat. "Very well, just have them back before tea."

"Very well indeed!" Sheridan said excitedly, inviting Letisha and Toby to climb onto his back. He stood on the porch looking out into the Otherworld. The landscape was green and beautiful. Mr Tempus and his wife stood in the doorway hand in hand. Sheridan checked everyone was secure, before jogging towards the edge of the porch and leaping over a newly fitted fence.

With Sheridan beating his shimmering wings, they took off into the clear blue heavens. Letisha held on tightly to the red scarf around his neck with Toby sat securely behind her. She decided that she could get used to being on time for everything; it had been the beginning of a most wonderful adventure. As they moved into the rising sun, she could not ignore the burning sensation she felt in her pocket. Father Time was a prisoner for now, but he was by no means defeated.

Letisha will return in book two of
The Fourth Ouroboros Anthology

THE
PORTAL
MAKER

ABOUT THE AUTHOR

Krista Joy is a writer and illustrator living in the West Midlands, England. She has been writing seriously since the age of fourteen, but doesn't do much else seriously. Her preferred title is The Mixed Media Storyteller. She enjoys drinking tea, old photographs and collecting anything curious. She lives in South Staffordshire with her husband and their two children.

Dragons and Dreamsellers is her first novel for children.

ACKNOWLEDGEMENTS

Thanks to the listeners, the readers and the correctors.
I couldn't have done it without you.

Printed in Great Britain
by Amazon

43276057R00111